The Big Town

The Big Town

How I and the Mrs. Go to New York to See Life and Get Katie a Husband

Ring W. Lardner

Introduction by Ross K. Tangedal

Hastings College Press | Hastings, Nebraska

Introduction © 2020 by Hastings College Press

The Big Town © 1921 by Bobbs-Merrill. This book has fallen into the public domain and is no longer subject to copyright protection.

All rights reserved. No part of this book may be used or reproduced in any manner whatsoever without permission from the publisher, except in the case of brief quotations embodied in critical articles and reviews.

Production Staff

Sam Crossett

Alexandru Dan

Sydney Dexter

Erika Diaz

Sarah Knight

James Lapka

Hannah Meeske

ISBN-13: 978-1-942885-60-3

Contents

Introduction

Ross K. Tangedal

> "I just want to be where
> they's Life and fun; where we
> can meet real live people."
> —Ella Finch to her husband,
> Tom Finch

> "…and with two taxi drivers and the
> baggageman thronging the station
> platform we pulled out of South
> Bend and set forth to see Life."
> —Tom Finch

Ring Lardner (1885–1933) was a baseball writer, short story writer, and columnist who produced some of the most popular magazine work of the early twentieth century. Many of his short stories appeared in publications ranging from *The Saturday Evening Post* to *Cosmopolitan,* and his popular "Busher" baseball stories (eventually collected and published as *You Know Me Al* in 1916) set a new standard for how to represent American vernacular. Lardner's influence was far-reaching, as his name became synonymous with literary celebrity from coast to coast due to his wide syndication. Oak Park High School's Ernest Hemingway wrote stories under the pseudonym "Ring Lardner, Jr." for his school newspaper, and Lardner's stories were championed by H.L. Mencken, F. Scott Fitzgerald, and Virginia Woolf. His signature style, which oftentimes eschewed third-person omniscience in favor of a first-person account from a "wise boob," allowed Lardner to present the foibles and fantasies of his country with satire and humor. He was often compared to Mark Twain, and by the mid-1920s, the expectation of writing a novel began dominating the critical conversation about his skills.

Lardner never wrote a novel. In fact the closest he came to the form may have been *The Big Town* (Bobbs-Merrill, 1921), his short story cycle about Tom and Ella Finch's desire to "see Life" and get Ella's sister Katie a husband by moving to New York City from South Bend, Indiana. One frequent explanation for the lack of critical attention given to Lardner is that he never wrote seriously—meaning he never wrote a novel—and his work is generally considered light, comic, satiric (but not serious satire), and of its time. However, Lardner had more than an ear for regional dialogue, colloquial speech, and comic situations.

Born in Niles, Michigan, Lardner never forgot his home region. Though he belonged to the same category of writers who left their small-town trappings in search of Chicago's opportunities (Theodore Dreiser, Sherwood Anderson, and others), Lardner chose to consistently focus his writing on people, regardless of region. He was keen to unearth hypocrisy wherever it lived, and he attempted to show faithfully the kinds of people who succumb to opportunity, to tomfoolery, and to each other. Charles Holmes concludes that Lardner "was not a frustrated genius who turned out journalistic pieces with cynical indifference, but a scrupulous craftsman, a writer who was a master of his medium and who treated it with respect" (29). Lardner's attention to craft, language, and place allowed him to experiment with perspective and tone at both urban and rural levels. He knew that readers would know his characters, or as he referred to them, "his puppets," and his fiction relied heavily on an almost molecular connection to the American language.

Near the end of World War I, Lardner had come to be known primarily for his magazine work, which included his "You Know Me Al" baseball stories. Published by George H. Doran in 1916, *You Know Me Al* was followed by a trio of loosely related story collections for Bobbs-Merrill, including *Gullible's Travels, Etc.* (1917), *The Young Immigrunts* (1920), and *The Big Town* (1921). Each book featured previously written magazine material, with Lardner doing nothing more than authorizing their collection and publication. However, by the time Lardner published *The Big Town*, Sinclair Lewis's *Main Street* (1920) was the bestselling novel in the country. Though Lardner refused to associate himself with any literary movement, his attempt to deal (perhaps subconsciously) with the new direction the supposed "revolt from the village" school of writers had taken is evident in *The Big Town*. The stories featured in the collection were published in the *Saturday Evening Post* between March 1920 and May 1921, at a time when Lewis's novel was at its sales apex, and each of Lardner's episodes features the recurring narrator Tom Finch, another in a long line of the "wise boob" characters he had perfected with *Gullible's Travels, Etc.* and *You Know Me Al.* If ever Lardner had considered skewering both the village *and* the city, his stories in *The Big Town* certainly express that possibility.

In the first story, "Quick Returns," Finch relays that his story is "only a kid," referring to a newspaper clipping entitled "Hoosier Cleans Up in Wall Street." Lardner dissects the inner social climate of "the Big Town" (New York City, New York) as mercilessly as Sinclair Lewis attacked small-town ignorance in *Main Street* one year earlier. Lardner's short work represents a rebuttal to the "revolt from the village," though his answer subverts the common notion of leaving the village in favor of the city. Phonies, fakers, and liars populate the trains, hotels, and restaurants of Lardner's text yet all fall victim to the same ritual: moving from place to place, for the sake of moving. The perceived simplicity of small-town life belied the urban growth sweeping the country. Though, as Douglas Noverr argues, characters like the Finches (especially Ella) must learn to "accept and learn to live with the confusions, turn-arounds and switches in directions, and unpredictable relationships that urban life presents" (73), they also must find a language to describe their rural/urban malaise. Lardner's use of misspellings, poor grammar, and turns-of-phrase in Tom's speech patterns shows not his character's lack of intelligence, but his defense against change. Hundreds of Ella Finches in small towns like Niles, Michigan, began wondering if living in the city was more than just a dream. Would they "move to town" in search of something more? And likewise, hundreds of Tom Finches dealt with the dissatisfaction of having to uproot and relocate for the sake of a loved one's quest to *see life*. Lardner recognized this unique kind of driftlessness, and through his characters' vacuous search for home he interrogates the wandering and foolishness at the heart of the rural/urban divide evident at the turn of the twentieth century in the United States.

Life, to Ella Finch, is New York City. To Tom Finch, the move is off-kilter, as South Bend, Indiana, embodies the calm, contemplative life where the family could live comfortably on the $150,000 inheritance Ella and her sister Katie had received from their war-profiteer stepfather. Lardner biographer Donald Elder calls Finch "the wise boob for whom Ring had an admiration and sympathy: that shrewd, pungent, middle-class American with a good-natured cynicism and a gift for phrasemaking" (177–78). Lardner noted earlier that his "wise boob" character "leads a regular life; has regular friends and is perfectly content to wade through life in a regular way" (qtd. in Elder 137). However, Lardner's Finch possesses a charming quality, an irascible wit, and an even temperament. The comedy in his language allows readers to see the community from which he sprang. This contrasts with Carl Van Doren's description of Sinclair Lewis's towns in *Contemporary American Novelists* (1922):

> conquered and converted by the legions of mediocrity, and now, grown rich and vain, are setting out to carry the dingy banner, led by the booster's calliope and the evangelist's bass drum, farther than it has ever gone before—to make provincialism imperialistic; so that all the native and instinctive virtues, freedoms, powers must rally in their own defense. Mr. Lewis hates such dulness—the village virus—as the saints hate sin. (162)

Those same villages populate Lardner's stories, but instead of *hating* the dullness, Lardner uses the dullness for comedy, a connecting point to further analyze Americans and their shortcomings.

Near the conclusion of "Quick Returns," Finch offers one of his signature screwball descriptions after discovering his wife's dalliance with Francis Griffin (who was supposed to be fixed up with Katie), and Katie's subsequent reaction to the infidelity: "Well, I didn't know Francis' home address, and Wall Street don't run Sundays, so I spent the Sabbath training on a quart of rye that a bell hop picked up at a bargain sale somewhere for fifteen dollars. Mean wile Katie had been let in on the secret and staid in our room all day, moaning like a prune-fed calf" (29). He proceeds to pummel Francis, which is his definition of "a Hoosier cleaning up in Wall Street" (30), and he and the ladies move on in the next story, to the next faker, to the next upwardly mobile character. Elder argues that in *The Big Town,* "it is particularly among these drifting people that the bores, the poseurs, and the phonies flourish; as if the upheaval of a secure, well-founded prewar world had set loose upon society a horde of predatory migrants in search of easy success ... they are another symptom of the breaking up of American life that took place in the twenties" (180). Finch busts up one of the poseurs, but his wife and sister-in-law ache to be part of that world, a world of rootless postwar royalty searching not for meaning, but for fleeting success.

The conclusion to "Quick Returns" revels in double-meanings, twisted syntax, and animadversions, all meant to satirize Prohibition, the middle-class, the *nouveau riche,* and sentimentality. Finch inhabits the mindset of a man both loyal to and repulsed by his wife and her actions, and his refusal to completely engage in her and Katie's adventures—he goes through the first story described multiple times as being dressed like "a South Bend embalmer"—is trumped by his duty to defend his pride by busting up Francis for kissing his wife. It is the in-between where Lardner does his damage as a satirist. Not only is he able to see through Ella and Katie's vapid search for a new life (read "home") in the big city, but he is also able to tease out a healthy cynicism from Tom. At one point, Finch criticizes the tepid stasis of South Bend: "between you and I the people we'd always ran round with was birds that was ready for bed as soon as they got home from the first show, and even though it had been printed in the News-Times that we had fell heir to a lot of jack we didn't have to hire no extra clerical help to tend to invitations received from the demi-Monday" (5). He also pokes fun at the landscape as the train takes his family to the Big Town: "Katie had brought a flock of magazines and started in on one of them at Elkhart, but it's pretty tough trying to read with the Northern Indiana mountains to look out at" (10). There are no mountains in Northern Indiana.

Finch does try to convince his wife that the move would be problematic: "So I argued and tried to compromise on somewheres in America, but it was New York or nothing with her. You see, she hadn't never been here, and all as she knew about it she'd read in books and magazines, and for some reason another when authors starts in on that subject it ain't very long till they've got a weeping jag" (9). Tom suggests a national boundary between New York City and America. He remarks that after meeting Francis Griffin and drinking a bottle of bourbon together in the washroom, "we was pretty near ready to forget national boundaries and kiss" (16). Lardner critiques the rural/urban divide in a succinct manner, and he offers a clear way to read *The Big Town* as a Midwestern text concerned with home and security. Lardner lets his readers see the disgust for region in Ella ("real" people live in New York City; "embalmers" live in South Bend), the indifference to region in Tom ("What I'm looking for is a home with a couple of beds and a cookstove in the kitchen, and maybe a bath" [15]), and the obliviousness in Katie (she pines over six men in the course of five stories). The characters take on these traits throughout the book, and each character sees the concept of "home" differently. For instance, Katie, after losing another suitor in "Lady Perkins," is distraught not from losing her beau in an airplane crash before he was able to sell his airplane for a million dollars, but from losing her potential home: "'No,' said Ella. 'Sis is taking it pretty calm. She's sensible. She says if that could of happened, why the invention couldn't of been no good after all. And the Williamses probably wouldn't of give him a plugged dime for it'" (83). Katie wants to acquire a home, a place of financial security unlike anything in South Bend, yet she falls for a charlatan Wall Street clerk posing as a banker in "Quick Returns," a rich, old man's married chauffeur in "Ritchey," a pilot with the potential for big money (until he dies) in "Lady Perkins," a jockey and a stable owner (in a world built on risk rather than security) in "Only One," and a comedian who marries her for *her* money in "Katie Wins a Home." By the final story, Katie becomes the financial security at the heart of her definition of home, an ironic twist crucial to Lardner's vision of America.

Likewise, Ella and Tom find themselves on a dual-quest, to see "life" and to get Katie a husband. Lardner showcases the lack of what Ella calls "home" in *The Big Town*. Case in point, when the three move into the Hotel Decker in "Lady Perkins," Tom characterizes the community at the heart of the hotel:

> Saturday nights everybody puts on their evening clothes like something was going to happen. But it don't. Sunday mornings the husbands and bachelors gets up earlier than usual to go to their real business, which is golf. The womenfolks are in full possession of the hotel till Sunday night supper and wives and husbands don't see one another all day long, but it don't seem as long as if they did. (62)

Ella's descriptions of South Bend reflect a similar monotony, where there are no "real" men for Katie to marry, where the three of them were "having pretty near as good a time as a bird with habitual boils" (8), where they were "acquainted there with the kind of people that makes it impossible for us to get acquainted with the other kind" (8). Tom tries to rectify their rootlessness: "the hotel's got all the modern conveniences like artificial light and a stopper in the bathtubs. They even got a barber and a valet, but you can't get a shave wile he's pressing your clothes, so it's pretty near impossible for a man to look their best at the same time" (62). For Finch, there is no way to be completely happy, and that comes at the expense of his wife's *nouveau riche* identity. The two eventually return to South Bend, but only after seeing Katie's definition of home rejected. Ella never experiences a home while in New York City, as is evidenced by her desire to move whenever conditions do not meet her imagined expectations. Her longing, coupled with Tom's dismissive comedy and Katie's eventual defeat, mark the book as a satire of upward-mobility. *The Big Town* shows readers just how ridiculous an imagined home can be when faced with expectations, visions of grandeur, and the need for more in an ethically despondent, postwar America.

In an ironic twist, the Finches (sans Katie) return to South Bend by the end of the book, with Finch declaring, "Do you remember what we moved to the Big Town for? We done it to see Life and get Katie a husband. Well, we got her a kind of a husband and I'll tell the world we seen Life. How about moseying back to South Bend?" (151). Ella, obviously dejected from their failed experiment as New Yorkers, reminds her husband, "But we haven't no home there now," to which Tom replies, "Nor we ain't had none since we left there" (151). In a "home is where the heart is" / "there's no place like home," moment, Tom reminds his wife and readers that the search for home (and prosperity) is as fruitless as betting on an injured show pony. Lardner never intended to write serious, long-form fiction, and he never did. However, the central search for home at the heart of *The Big Town* amplifies his strengths as a cultural commentator, albeit a reluctant one.

Finch finally declares, after he and Ella return to South Bend: "So here we are, really enjoying ourselfs for the first time in pretty near two years. And Katie's in New York, enjoying herself, too, I suppose. She ought to be, married to a comedian. It must be such fun to just set and listen to him talk" (151). In somewhat prophetic terms, Lardner describes himself in the world of literature at the time (and for all time). His stories were, on the surface, read as light comedy spread out across countless situations. But beneath the fun can be found a clear-eyed observer of the witless yearning to move up, to succeed in a big way, to become more than meets the eye. There is no home in Ring Lardner's *The Big Town,* but his characters' frustrating search to define, secure, and maintain "home" speaks to a Midwest American identity more complicated than a revolting villager, and more complex than a starry-eyed wanderer.

Works Cited

Elder, Donald. *Ring Lardner: A Biography.* Doubleday & Company, Inc., 1956.

Holmes, Charles S. "Ring Lardner: Reluctant Artist." *A Question of Quality: Popularity and Value in Modern Creative*

Writing. Edited by Louis Filler, Bowling Green State University Popular Press, 1976, pp. 26–39

Lardner, Ring. *The Big Town*. [1921]. Hastings College Press, 2020.

Noverr, Douglas A. "The Small Town and the Urban Midwest in Ring Lardner's *You Know Me Al*." *MidAmerica* vol. 25, 1998, pp. 68–77.

Van Doren, Carl. *Contemporary American Novelists, 1900–1922*. Macmillan, 1922.

....

Ross K. Tangedal is Assistant Professor of English and Director of the Cornerstone Press at the University of Wisconsin–Stevens Point. He is the author of *The Preface: American Authorship in the Twentieth Century* (Palgrave Macmillan 2021) and co-editor (with Joshua M. Murray) of *Editing the Harlem Renaissance* (Clemson University Press 2021). He specializes in American print and publishing culture, textual editing, bibliography, and book history. His work on Lardner has been published in *Authorship* and reprinted in *Twentieth Century Literary Criticism*.

I

QUICK RETURNS

This is just a clipping from one of the New York papers; a little kidding piece that they had in about me two years ago. It says:

> Hoosier Cleans Up in Wall Street. Employees of the brokerage firm of H.L. Krause & Co. are authority for the statement that a wealthy Indiana speculator made one of the biggest killings of the year in the Street yesterday afternoon. No very definite information was obtainable, as the Westerner's name was known to only one of the firm's employees, Francis Griffin, and he was unable to recall it last night.

You'd think I was a millionaire and that I'd made a sucker out of Morgan or something, but it's only kid, see? If they'd of printed the true story they wouldn't of had no room left for that day's selections at Pimlico, and God knows that would of been fatal.

But if you want to hear about it, I'll tell you.

Well, the war wound up in the fall of 1918. The only member of my family that was killed in it was my wife's stepfather. He died of grief when it ended with him two hundred thousand dollars ahead. I immediately had a black bandage sewed round my left funny bone, but when they read us the will I felt all right again and tore it off. Our share was seventy-five thousand dollars. This was after we had paid for the inheritance tax and the amusement stamps on a horseless funeral.

My young sister-in-law, Katie, dragged down another seventy-five thousand dollars and the rest went to the old bird that had been foreman in papa's factory. This old geezer had been starving to death for twenty years on the wages my stepfather-in-law give him, and the rest of us didn't make no holler when his name was read off for a small chunk, especially as he didn't have no teeth to enjoy it with.

I could of had this old foreman's share, maybe, if I'd of took advantage of the offer "father" made me just before his daughter and I was married. I was over in Niles, Michigan, where they lived, and he insisted on me seeing his factory, which meant smelling it too. At that time I was knocking out about eighteen hundred dollars per annum selling cigars out of South Bend, and the old man said he would start me in with him at only about a fifty per cent cut, but we would also have the privilege of living with him and my wife's kid sister.

"They's a lot to be learnt about this business," he says, "but if you would put your mind on it you might work up to manager. Who knows?"

"My nose knows," I said, and that ended it

The old man had lost some jack and went into debt a good many years ago, and for a long wile before the war begin about all as he was able to do was support himself and the two gals and pay off a part of what he owed. When the war broke loose and leather went up to hell and gone I and my wife thought he would get prosperous, but before this country went in his business went on about the same as usual.

"I don't know how they do it," he would say. "Other leather men is getting rich on contracts with the Allies, but I can't land a one."

I guess he was trying to sell razor strops to Russia.

Even after we got into it and he begin to clean up, with the factory running day and night, all as we knew was that he had contracts with the U.S. Government, but he never confided in us what special stuff he was turning out. For all as we knew, it may of been medals for the ground navy.

Anyway, he must of been hitting a fast clip when the armistice come and ended the war for everybody but Congress!

It's a cinch he wasn't amongst those arrested for celebrating too loud on the night of November 11. On the contrary they tell me that when the big news hit Niles the old bird had a stroke that he didn't never recover from, and though my wife and Katie hung round the bedside day after day in the hopes he would tell how much he was going to leave he was keeping his fiscal secrets for Oliver Lodge or somebody, and it wasn't till we seen the will that we knew we wouldn't have to work no more, which is pretty fair consolation even for the loss of a stepfather-in-law that ran a perfume mill.

"Just think," said my wife, "after all his financial troubles, papa died a rich man!"

"Yes," I said to myself, "and a patriot. His only regret was that he just had one year to sell leather to his country."

If the old codger had of only been half as fast a salesman as his two daughters this clipping would of been right when it called me a wealthy Hoosier. It wasn't two weeks after we seen the will when the gals had disposed of the odor factory and the old home in Niles, Michigan. Katie, it seemed, had to come over to South Bend and live with us. That was agreeable to me, as I figured that if two could live on eighteen hundred dollars a year three could struggle along some way on the income off one hundred and fifty thousand dollars.

Only for me, though, Ella and Sister Kate would of shot the whole wad into a checking account so as the bank could enjoy it wile it lasted. I argued and fought and finally persuaded them to keep five thousand apiece for pin money and stick the rest into bonds.

The next thing they done was run over to Chi and buy all the party dresses that was vacant. Then they come back to South Bend and wished somebody would give a party. But between you and I the people we'd always ran round with was birds that was ready for bed as soon as they got home from the first show, and even though it had been printed in the News-Times that we had fell heir to a lot of jack we didn't have to hire no extra clerical help to tend to invitations received from the demi-Monday.

Finally Ella said we would start something ourselves. So she got a lot of invitations printed and sent them to all our friends that could read and hired a cater and a three-piece orchestra and everything, and made me buy a dress suit.

Well, the big night arrived and everybody come that had somebody to leave their baby with. The hosts wore evening clothes and the rest of the merrymakers prepared for the occasion with a shine or a clean collar. At first the cat had everybody's tongue, but when we sat down to eat some of the men folks begun to get comical. For instance, they would say to my wife or Katie, "Ain't you afraid you'll catch cold?" And they'd say to me, "I didn't know you was a waiter at the Oliver." Before the fish course everybody was in a fair way to get the giggles.

After supper the musicians come and hid behind a geranium and played a jazz. The entire party set out the first dance. The second was a solo between Katie and I, and I had the third with my wife. Then Kate and the Mrs. had one together, wile I tried holds with a lady named Mrs. Eckhart, who seemed to think that somebody had ast her to stand for a time exposure. The men folks had all drifted over behind the plant to watch the drummer, but after the stalemate between Mrs. Eckhart and I, I grabbed her husband and took him out in the kitchen and showed him a bottle of bourbon that I'd been saving for myself, in the hopes it would loosen him up. I told him it was my last bottle, but he must of thought I said it was the last bottle in the world. Anyway, when he got through they was international prohibition.

We went back in the ballroom and sure enough he ast Katie to dance. But he hadn't no sooner than win one fall when his wife challenged him to take her home and that started the epidemic that emptied the house of everybody but the orchestra and us. The orchestra had been hired to stay till midnight, which was still two hours and a half distance, so I invited both of the gals to dance with me at once, but it seems like they was surfeited with that sport and wanted to cry a little. Well, the musicians had ran out of blues, so I chased them home.

"Some party!" I said, and the two girls give me a dirty look like it was my fault or something. So we all went to bed and the ladies beat me to it on account of being so near ready.

Well, they wasn't no return engagements even hinted at and the only other times all winter when the gals had a chance to dress up was when some secondhand company would come to town with a show and I'd have to buy a box. We couldn't ask nobody to go with us on account of not having no friends that you could depend on to not come in their stocking feet.

Finally it was summer and the Mrs. said she wanted to get out of town.

"We've got to be fair to Kate," she said.

"We don't know no young unmarried people in South Bend and it's no fun for a girl to run round with her sister and brother-in-law. Maybe if we'd go to some resort somewheres we might get acquainted with people that could show her a good time."

So I hired us rooms in a hotel down to Wawasee Lake and we stayed there from the last of June till the middle of September. During that time I caught a couple of bass and Kate caught a couple of carp from Fort Wayne. She was getting pretty friendly with one of them when along come a wife that he hadn't thought was worth mentioning. The other bird was making a fight against the gambling fever, but one night it got the best of him and he dropped forty-five cents in the nickel machine and had to go home and make a new start.

About a week before we was due to leave I made the remark that it would seem good to be back in South Bend and get some home cooking.

"Listen!" says my wife. "I been wanting for a long wile to have a serious talk with you and now's as good a time as any. Here are I and Sis and you with an income of over eight thousand dollars a year and having pretty near as good a time as a bird with habitual boils. What's more, we can't never have a good time in South Bend, but have got to move somewheres where we are unknown."

"South Bend is certainly all of that," I said.

"No, it isn't," said the Mrs. "We're acquainted there with the kind of people that makes it impossible for us to get acquainted with the other kind. Kate could live there twenty years and never meet a decent man. She's a mighty attractive girl, and if she had a chance they's nobody she couldn't marry. But she won't never have a chance in South Bend. And they's no use of you saying 'Let her move,' because I'm going to keep her under my eye till she's married and settled down. So in other words, I want us to pack up and leave South Bend for good and all and move somewheres where we'll get something for our money."

"For instance, where?" I ast her.

"They's only one place," she said; "New York City."

"I've heard of it," said I, "but I never heard that people who couldn't enjoy themselves on eight thousand a year in South Bend could go to New York and tear it wide open."

"I'm not planning to make no big splurge," she says. "I just want to be where they's Life and fun; where we can meet real live people. And as for not living there on eight thousand, think of the families that's already living there on half of that and less!"

"And think of the Life and fun they're having!" I says.

"But when you talk about eight thousand a year," said the Mrs., "why do we have to hold ourselves to that? We can sell some of those bonds and spend a little of our principal. It will just be taking money out of one investment and putting it in another."

"What other?" I ast her.

"Kate," said the wife. "You let me take her to New York and manage her and I'll get her a husband that'll think our eight thousand a year fell out of his vest."

"Do you mean," I said, "that you'd let a sister of yours marry for money?"

"Well," she says, "I know a sister of hers that wouldn't mind if she had."

So I argued and tried to compromise on somewheres in America, but it was New York or nothing with her. You see, she hadn't never been here, and all as she knew about it she'd read in books and magazines, and for some reason another when authors starts in on that subject it ain't very long till they've got a weeping jag. Besides, what chance did I have when she kept reminding me that it was her stepfather, not mine, that had croaked and made us all rich?

When I had give up she called Kate in and told her, and Kate squealed and kissed us both, though God knows I didn't deserve no remuneration or ask for none.

Ella had things all planned out. We was to sell our furniture and take a furnished apartment here, but we would stay in some hotel till we found a furnished apartment that was within reason.

"Our stay in some hotel will be lifelong," I said.

The furniture, when we come to sell it, wasn't worth nothing, and that's what we got. We didn't have nothing to ship, as Ella found room for our books in my collar box. I got two lowers and an upper in spite of the Government, and with two taxi drivers and the baggageman thronging the station platform we pulled out of South Bend and set forth to see Life.

The first four miles of the journey was marked by considerable sniveling on the part of the heiresses.

"If it's so painful to leave the Bend, let's go back," I said.

"It isn't leaving the Bend," said the Mrs., "but it makes a person sad to leave any place."

"Then we're going to have a muggy trip," said I. "This train stops pretty near everywheres to either discharge passengers or employees."

They were still sobbing when we left Mishawaka and I had to pull some of my comical stuff to get their minds off. My wife's mighty easy to look at when she hasn't got those watery blues, but I never did see a gal that knocked you for a goal when her nose was in full bloom.

Katie had brought a flock of magazines and started in on one of them at Elkhart, but it's pretty tough trying to read with the Northern Indiana mountains to look out at, to say nothing about the birds of prey that kept prowling up and down the aisle in search of a little encouragement or a game of rhum.

I noticed a couple of them that would of give a lady an answer if she'd approached them in a nice way, but I've done some traveling myself and I know what kind of men it is that allows themselves to be drawed into a flirtation on trains. Most of them has made the mistake of getting married some time, but they don't tell you that. They tell you that you and a gal they use to be stuck on is as much alike as a pair of corsets, and if you ever come to Toledo to give them a ring, and they hand you a telephone number that's even harder to get than the ones there are; and they ask you your name and address and write it down, and the next time they're up at the Elks they show it to a couple of the brothers and tell what they'd of done if they'd only been going all the way through.

"Say, I hate to talk about myself! But say!"

Well, I didn't see no sense in letting Katie waste her time on those kind of guys, so every time one of them looked our way I give him the fish eye and the non-stop signal. But this was my first long trip since the Government started to play train, and I didn't know the new rules in regards to getting fed; otherwise I wouldn't of never cleaned up in Wall Street

In the old days we use to wait till the boy come through and announced that dinner was now being served in the dining car forward; then we'd saunter into the washroom and wash our hands if necessary, and ramble into the diner and set right down and enjoy as big a meal as we could afford. But the Government wants to be economical, so they've cut down the number of trains, to say nothing about the victuals; and they's two or three times as many people traveling, because they can't throw their money away fast enough at home. So the result is that the wise guys keeps an eye on their watch and when it's about twenty minutes to dinner time they race to the diner and park against the door and get quick action; and after they've eat the first time they go out and stand in the vestibule and wait till it's their turn again, as one Federal meal don't do nothing to your appetite only whet it, you might say.

Well, anyway, I was playing the old rules and by the time I and the two gals started for the diner we run up against the outskirts of a crowd pretty near as big as the ones that waits outside restaurant windows to watch a pancake turn turtle. About eight o'clock we got to where we could see the wealthy dining car conductor in the distance, but it was only about once every quarter of an hour that he raised a hand, and then he seemed to of had all but one of his fingers shot off.

I have often heard it said that the way to a man's heart is through his stomach, but every time I ever seen men and women keep waiting for their eats it was always the frail sex that give the first yelp, and personally I've often wondered what would of happened in the trenches Over There if ladies had of been occupying them when the rations failed to show up. I guess the bombs bursting round would of sounded like Sweet and Low sang by a quextette of deef mutes.

Anyway, my two charges was like wild animals, and when the con finally held up two fingers I didn't have no more chance or desire to stop them than as if they was the Center College Football Club right after opening prayer.

The pair of them was ushered to a table for four where they already was a couple of guys making the best of it, and it wasn't more than ten minutes later when one of these birds dipped his bill in the finger bowl and staggered out, but by the time I took his place the other gent and my two gals was talking like barbers.

The guy was Francis Griffin that's in the clipping. But when Ella introduced us all as she said was, "This is my husband," without mentioning his name, which she didn't know at that time, or mine, which had probably slipped her memory.

Griffin looked at me like I was a side dish that he hadn't ordered. Well, I don't mind snubs except when I get them, so I ast him if he wasn't from Sioux City—you could tell he was from New York by his blue collar.

"From Sioux City!" he says. "I should hope not!"

"I beg your pardon," I said. "You look just like a photographer I used to know out there."

"I'm a New Yorker," he said, "and I can't get home too soon."

"Not on this train, you can't," I said.

"I missed the Century," he says.

"Well," I says with a polite smile, "the Century's loss is our gain."

"Your wife's been telling me," he says, "that you're moving to the Big Town. Have you ever been there?"

"Only for a few hours," I says.

"Well," he said, "when you've been there a few weeks you'll wonder why you ever lived anywhere else. When I'm away from old Broadway I always feel like I'm only camping out."

Both the gals smiled their appreciation, so I says: "That certainly expresses it. You'd ought to remember that line and give it to Georgie Cohan."

"Old Georgie!" he says. "I'd give him anything I got and welcome. But listen! Your wife mentioned something about a good hotel to stop at wile you're looking for a home. Take my advice and pick out one that's near the center of things; you'll more than make up the difference in taxi bills. I lived up in the Hundreds one winter and it averaged me ten dollars a day in cab fares."

"You must of had a pleasant home life," I says.

"Me!" he said. "I'm an old bachelor."

"Old!" says Kate, and her and the Mrs. both giggled.

"But seriously," he says, "if I was you I would go right to the Baldwin, where you can get a room for twelve dollars a day for the three of you; and you're walking distance from the theaters or shops or cafes or anywheres you want to go."

"That sounds grand!" said Ella.

"As far as I'm concerned," I said, "I'd just as lief be overseas from any of the places you've mentioned. What I'm looking for is a home with a couple of beds and a cookstove in the kitchen, and maybe a bath."

"But we want to see New York first," said Katie, "and we can do that better without no household cares."

"That's the idear!" says Griffin. "Eat, drink and be merry; to-morrow we may die."

"I guess we won't drink ourselves to death," I said, "not if the Big Town's like where we been living."

"Oh, say!" says our new friend. "Do you think little old New York is going to stand for Prohibition? Why, listen! I can take you to thirty places to-morrow night where you can get all you want in any one of them."

"Let's pass up the other twenty-nine," I says.

"But that isn't the idear," he said. "What makes we New Yorkers sore is to think they should try and wish a law like that on Us. Isn't this supposed to be a government of the people, for the people and by the people?"

"People!" I said. "Who and the hell voted for Prohibition if it wasn't the people?"

"The people of where?" he says. "A lot of small-time hicks that couldn't buy a drink if they wanted it."

"Including the hicks," I says, "that's in the New York State legislature."

"But not the people of New York City," he said. "And you can't tell me it's fair to spring a thing like this without warning on men that's got their fortunes tied up in liquor that they can't never get rid of now, only at a sacrifice."

"You're right," I said. "They ought to give them some warning. Instead of that they was never even a hint of what was coming off till Maine went dry seventy years ago."

"Maine?" he said. "What the hell is Maine?"

"I don't know," I said. "Only they was a ship or a boat or something named after it once, and the Spaniards sunk it and we sued them for libel or something."

"You're a smart Aleck," he said. "But speaking about war, where was you?"

"In the shipyards at South Bend painting a duck boat," I says. "And where was you?"

"I'd of been in there in a few more weeks," he says. "They wasn't no slackers in the Big Town."

"No," said I, "and America will never forget New York for coming in on our side."

By this time the gals was both giving me dirty looks, and we'd eat all we could get, so we paid our checks and went back in our car and I felt kind of apologetic, so I dug down in the old grip and got out a bottle of bourbon that a South Bend pal of mine, George Hull, had give me the day before; and Griffin and I went in the wash-room with it and before the evening was over we was pretty near ready to forget national boundaries and kiss.

The old bourb' helped me save money the next morning, as I didn't care for no breakfast. Ella and Kate went in with Griffin and you could of knocked me over with a coupling pin when the Mrs. come back and reported that he'd insisted on paying the check. "He told us all about himself," she said. "His name is Francis Griffin and he's in Wall Street. Last year he cleared twenty thousand dollars in commissions and everything."

"He's a piker," I says. "Most of them never even think under six figures."

"There you go!" said the Mrs. "You never believe nothing. Why shouldn't he be telling the truth? Didn't he buy our breakfast?"

"I been buying your breakfast for five years," I said, "but that don't prove that I'm knocking out twenty thousand per annum in Wall Street."

Francis and Katie was setting together four or five seats ahead of us.

"You ought to of seen the way he looked at her in the diner," said the Mrs. "He looked like he wanted to eat her up."

"Everybody gets desperate in a diner these days," I said. "Did you and Kate go fifty-fifty with him? Did you tell him how much money we got?"

"I should say not!" says Ella. "But I guess we did say that you wasn't doing nothing just now and that we was going to New York to see Life, after being cooped up in a small town all these years. And Sis told him you'd made us put pretty near everything in bonds, so all we can spend is eight thousand a year. He said that wouldn't go very far in the Big Town."

"I doubt if it ever gets as far as the Big Town," I said. "It won't if he makes up his mind to take it away from us."

"Oh, shut up!" said the Mrs. "He's all right and I'm for him, and I hope Sis is too. They'd make a stunning couple. I wished I knew what they're talking about."

"Well," I said, "they're both so reserved that I suppose they're telling each other how they're affected by cucumbers."

When they come back and joined us Ella said: "We was just remarking how well you two young things seemed to be getting along. We was wondering what you found to say to one another all this time."

"Well," said Francis, "just now I think we were discussing you. Your sister said you'd been married five years and I pretty near felt like calling her a fibber. I told her you looked like you was just out of high school."

"I've heard about you New Yorkers before," said the Mrs. "You're always trying to flatter somebody."

"Not me," said Francis. "I never say nothing without meaning it."

"But sometimes," says I, "you'd ought to go on and explain the meaning."

Along about Schenectady my appetite begin to come back. I'd made it a point this time to find out when the diner was going to open, and then when it did our party fell in with the door.

"The wife tells me you're on the stock exchange," I says to Francis when we'd give our order.

"Just in a small way," he said. "But they been pretty good to me down there. I knocked out twenty thousand last year."

"That's what he told us this morning," said Ella.

"Well," said I, "they's no reason for a man to forget that kind of money between Rochester and Albany, even if this is a slow train."

"Twenty thousand isn't a whole lot in the Big Town," said Francis, "but still and all, I manage to get along and enjoy myself a little on the side."

"I suppose it's enough to keep one person," I said.

"Well," says Francis, "they say two can live as cheap as one."

Then him and Kate and Ella all giggled, and the waiter brought in a part of what he thought we'd ordered and we eat what we could and ast for the check. Francis said he wanted it and I was going to give in to him after a long hard struggle, but the gals reminded him that he'd paid for breakfast, so he said all right, but we'd all have to take dinner with him some night.

I and Francis set a wile in the washroom and smoked, and then he went to entertain the gals, but I figured the wife would go right to sleep like she always does when they's any scenery to look out at, so I stuck where I was and listened to what a couple of toothpick salesmen from Omsk would of done with the League of Nations if Wilson had of had sense enough to leave it to them.

Pulling into the Grand Central Station, Francis apologized for not being able to steer us over to the Baldwin and see us settled, but said he had to rush right downtown and report on his Chicago trip before the office closed. To see him when he parted with the gals you'd of thought he was going clear to Siberia to compete in the Olympic Games, or whatever it is we're in over there.

Well, I took the heiresses to the Baldwin and got a regular Big Town welcome. Ella and Kate set against a pillar wile I tried different tricks to make an oilhaired clerk look at me. New York hotel clerks always seem to of just dropped something and can't take their eyes off the floor. Finally I started to pick up the register and the guy give me the fish eye and ast what he could do for me.

"Well," I said, "when I come to a hotel I don't usually want to buy a straw hat."

He ast me if I had a reservation and I told him no.

"Can't do nothing for you then," he says. "Not till to-morrow morning anyway."

So I went back to the ladies.

"We'll have to go somewheres else," I said. "This joint's a joint. They won't give us nothing till to-morrow."

"But we can't go nowheres else," said the Mrs. "What would Mr. Griffin think, after recommending us to come here?"

"Well," I said, "if you think I'm going to park myself in a four-post chair all night just because we got a tip on a hotel from Wall Street you're Queen of the Cuckoos."

"Are you sure they haven't anything at all?" she says.

"Go ask them yourself!" I told her.

Well, she did, and in about ten minutes she come back and said everything was fixed.

"They'll give us a single room with bath and a double room with bath for fifteen dollars a day," she said.

"'Give us' is good!" said I.

"I told him we'd wired for reservations and it wasn't our fault if the wire didn't get here," she said. "He was awfully nice."

Our rooms was right close to each other on the twenty-first floor. On the way up we decided by two votes to one that we'd dress for dinner. I was still monkeying with my tie when Katie come in for Ella to look her over. She had on the riskiest dress she'd bought in Chi.

"It's a pretty dress," she said, "but I'm afraid maybe it's too daring for just a hotel dining room."

Say, we hadn't no sooner than set down in the hotel dining room when two other gals come in that made my team look like they was dressed for a sleigh ride with Doc Cook.

"I guess you don't feel so daring now," I said. "Compared to that baby in black you're wearing Jess Willard's ulster."

"Do you know what that black gown cost?" said Ella. "Not a cent under seven hundred dollars."

"That would make the material twenty-one hundred dollars a yard," I says.

"I'd like to know where she got it," said Katie.

"Maybe she cut up an old stocking," said I.

"I wished now," said the Mrs., "that we'd waited till we got here before we bought our clothes."

"You can bet one thing," says Katie. "Before we're ast out anywheres on a real party we'll have something to wear that isn't a year old."

"First thing to-morrow morning," says the Mrs., "we'll go over on Fifth Avenue and see what we can see."

"They'll only be two on that excursion," I says.

"Oh, we don't want you along," said Ella. "But I do wished you'd go to some first-class men's store and get some ties and shirts and things that don't look like an embalmer."

Well, after a wile one of the waiters got it in his head that maybe we hadn't came in to take a bath, so he fetched over a couple of programs.

"Never mind them," I says. "What's ready? We're in a hurry."

"The Long Island Duckling's very nice," he said. "And how about some nice au gratin potatoes and some nice lettuce and tomato salad with Thousand Island dressing, and maybe some nice French pastry?"

"Everything seems to be nice here," I said. "But wait a minute. How about something to drink?"

He give me a mysterious smile.

"Well," he said, "they're watching us pretty close here, but we serve something we call a cup. It comes from the bar and we're not supposed to know what the bartender puts in it."

"We'll try and find out," I said. "And rush this order through, as we're starved."

So he frisked out and was back again in less than an hour with another guy to help carry the stuff, though Lord knows he could of parked the three ducklings on one eyelid and the whole meal on the back of his hand. As for the cup, when you tasted it they wasn't no big mystery about what the bartender had put in it—a bottle of seltzer and a prune and a cherry and an orange peel, and maybe his finger. The check come to eighteen dollars and Ella made me tip him the rest of a twenty.

Before dinner the gals had been all for staying up a wile and looking the crowd over, but when we was through they both owned up that they hadn't slept much on the train and was ready for bed.

Ella and Kate was up early in the morning. They had their breakfast without me and went over to stun Fifth Avenue. About ten o'clock Francis phoned to say he'd call round for us that evening and take us to dinner. The gals didn't get back till late in the afternoon, but from one o'clock on I was too busy signing for packages to get lonesome. Ella finally staggered in with some more and I told her about our invitation.

"Yes, I know," she said.

"How do you know?" I ast her.

"He told us," she said. "We had to call him up to get a check cashed."

"You got plenty nerve!" I said. "How does he know your checks is good?"

"Well, he likes us," she said. "You'll like us too when you see us in some of the gowns we bought."

"Some!" I said.

"Why, yes," said the Mrs. "You don't think a girl can go round in New York with one evening dress!"

"How much money did you spend today?" I ast her.

"Well," she said, "things are terribly high—that is, nice things. And then, of course, there's suits and hats and things besides the gowns. But remember, it's our money. And as I told you, it's an investment. When young Mister Wall Street sees Kate to-night it'll be all off."

"I didn't call on you for no speech," I says. "I ast you how much you spent."

"Not quite sixteen hundred dollars." I was still out on my feet when the phone rung. Ella answered it and then told me it was all right about the tickets.

"What tickets?" I said.

"Why, you see," she says, "after young Griffin fixing us up with that check and inviting us to dinner and everything we thought it would be nice to take him to a show to-night. Kate wanted to see Ups and Downs, but the girl said she couldn't get us seats for it. So I ast that nice clerk that took care of us yesterday and he's fixed it."

"All right," I said, "but when young Griffin starts a party, why and the hell not let him finish it?"

"I suppose he would of took us somewheres after dinner," says the Mrs., "but I couldn't be sure. And between you and I, I'm positive that if he and Kate is throwed together a whole evening, and her looking like she'll look to-night, we'll get mighty quick returns on our investment."

Well, to make a short story out of it, the gals finally got what they called dressed, and I wished Niles, Michigan, or South Bend could of seen them. If boxers wore bathing skirts I'd of thought I was in the ring with a couple of bantams.

"Listen!" I said. "What did them two girdles cost?"

"Mine was three hundred and Kate's three hundred and fifty," said the Mrs.

"Well," I says, "don't you know that you could of went to any cut-rate drug store and wrapped yourself up just as warm in thirty-two cents' worth of adhesive tape? Listen!" I said. "What's the use of me paying a burglar for tickets to a show like Ups and Downs when I could set round here and look at you for nothing?"

Then Griffin rung up to say that he was waiting and we went downstairs. Francis took us in the same dining room we'd been in the night before, but this time the waiters all fought each other to get to us first.

I don't know what we eat, as Francis had something on the hip that kind of dazed me for a wile, but afterwards I know we got a taxi and went to the theater. The tickets was there in my name and only cost me thirteen dollars and twenty cents.

Maybe you seen this show wile it was here. Some show! I didn't read the program to see who wrote it, but I guess the words was by Noah and the music took the highest awards at the St. Louis Fair. They had a good system on the gags. They didn't spring none but what you'd heard all your life and knew what was coming, so instead of just laughing at the point you laughed all the way through it.

I said to Ella, I said, "I bet the birds that run this don't want prohibition. If people paid $3.30 apiece and come in here sober they'd come back the next night with a machine gun."

"I think it's dandy," she says, "and you'll notice every seat is full. But listen! Will you do something for me? When this is over suggest that we go up to the Castle Roof for a wile."

"What for?" I said. "I'm sleepy."

"Just this once," she says. "You know what I told you about quick returns!"

Well, I give in and made the suggestion, and I never seen people so easy coaxed. I managed to get a ringside table for twenty-two bucks. Then I ast the boy how about getting a drink and he ast me if I knew any of the head waiters.

"I do," says Francis. "Tell Hector it's for Frank Griffin's party."

So we ordered four Scotch highballs and some chicken à la King, and then the dinge orchestra tore loose some jazz and I was expecting a dance with Ella, but before she could ask me Francis had ast her, and I had one with Kate.

"Your Wall Street friend's a fox," I says, "asking an old married lady to dance so's to stand in with the family."

"Old married lady!" said Kate. "Sis don't look a day over sixteen to-night."

"How are you and Francis coming?" I ast her.

"I don't know," she says. "He acts kind of shy. He hasn't hardly said a word to me all evening."

Well, they was another jazz and I danced it with Ella; then her and Francis had another one and I danced again with Kate. By this time our food and refreshments was served and the show was getting ready to start.

I could write a book on what I don't remember about that show. The first sip of their idear of a Scotch highball put me down for the count of eight and I was practic'lly unconscious till the waiter woke me up with a check for forty bucks.

Francis seen us home and said he would call up again soon, and when Ella and I was alone I made the remark that I didn't think he'd ever strain his larnix talking to Kate.

"He acts gun-shy when he's round her," I says. "You seem to be the one that draws him out."

"It's a good sign," she says. "A man's always embarrassed when he's with a girl he's stuck on. I'll bet you anything you want to bet that within a week something'll happen."

Well, she win. She'd of win if she'd of said three days instead of a week. It was a Wednesday night when we had that party, and on the Friday Francis called up and said he had tickets for the Palace. I'd been laid up mean wile with the Scotch influenza, so I told the gals to cut me out. I was still awake yet when Ella come in a little after midnight.

"Well," I said, "are we going to have a brother-in-law?"

"Mighty soon," she says.

So I ast her what had came off.

"Nothing—to-night," she says, "except this: He wrote me a note. He wants me to go with him to-morrow afternoon and look at a little furnished apartment. And he ast me if I could come without Sis, as he wants to pull a surprise on her. So I wondered if you couldn't think of some way to fix it so's I can sneak off for a couple of hours."

"Sure!" I said. "Just tell her you didn't sleep all night and you're wore out and you want to take a nap."

So she pulled this gag at lunch Saturday and Katie said she was tired too. She went up to her room and Ella snuck out to keep her date with Francis. In less than an hour she romped into our room again and throwed herself on the bed.

"Well," I says, "it must of been a little apartment if it didn't only take you this long to see it."

"Oh, shut up!" she said. "I didn't see no apartment. And don't say a word to me or I'll scream."

Well, I finally got her calmed down and she give me the details. It seems that she'd met Francis, and he'd got a taxi and they'd got in the taxi and they hadn't no sooner than got in the taxi when Francis give her a kiss.

"Quick returns," I says.

"I'll kill you if you say another word!" she says.

So I managed to keep still.

Well, I didn't know Francis' home address, and Wall Street don't run Sundays, so I spent the Sabbath training on a quart of rye that a bell hop picked up at a bargain sale somewheres for fifteen dollars. Mean wile Katie had been let in on the secret and staid in our room all day, moaning like a prune-fed calf.

"I'm afraid to leave her alone," says Ella. "I'm afraid she'll jump out the window."

"You're easily worried," I said. "What I'm afraid of is that she won't."

Monday morning finally come, as it generally always does, and I told the gals I was going to some first-class men's store and buy myself some ties and shirts that didn't look like a South Bend embalmer.

So the only store I knew about was H.L. Krause & Co. in Wall Street, but it turned out to be an office. I ast for Mr. Griffin and they ast me my name and I made one up, Sam Hall or something, and out he come.

If I told you the rest of it you'd think I was bragging. But I did bust a few records. Charley Brickley and Walter Eckersall both kicked five goals from field in one football game, and they was a bird named Robertson or something out at Purdue that kicked seven. Then they was one of the old-time ball players, Bobby Lowe or Ed Delehanty, that hit four or five home runs in one afternoon. And out to Toledo that time Dempsey made big Jess set down seven times in one round.

Well, listen! In a little less than three minutes I floored this bird nine times and I kicked him for eight goals from the field and I hit him over the fence for ten home runs. Don't talk records to me!

So that's what they meant in the clipping about a Hoosier cleaning up in Wall Street. But it's only a kid, see?

II

RITCHEY

Well, I was just getting used to the Baldwin and making a few friends round there when Ella suddenly happened to remember that it was Griffin who had recommended it. So one day, wile Kate was down to the chiropodist's, Ella says it was time for us to move and she had made up her mind to find an apartment somewheres.

"We could get along with six rooms," she said. "All as I ask is for it to be a new building and on some good street, some street where the real people lives."

"You mean Fifth Avenue," said I.

"Oh, no," she says. "That's way over our head. But we'd ought to be able to find something, say, on Riverside Drive."

"A six room apartment," I says, "in a new building on Riverside Drive? What was you expecting to pay?"

"Well," she said, "you remember that time I and Kate visited the Kitchells in Chi? They had a dandy apartment on Sheridan Road, six rooms and brand new. It cost them seventy-five dollars a month. And Sheridan Road is Chicago's Riverside Drive."

"Oh, no," I says. "Chicago's Riverside Drive is Canal Street. But listen: Didn't the Kitchells have their own furniture?"

"Sure they did," said Ella.

"And are you intending to furnish us all over complete?" I asked her.

"Of course not," she says. "I expect to get a furnished apartment. But that don't only make about twenty-five dollars a month difference."

"Listen," I said: "It was six years ago that you visited the Kitchells; beside which, that was Chi and this is the Big Town. If you find a six room furnished apartment for a hundred dollars in New York City to-day, we'll be on Pell Street in Chinatown, and maybe Katie can marry into a laundry or a joss house."

"Well," said the wife, "even if we have to go to $150 a month for a place on the Drive, remember half of it's my money and half of it's Kate's, and none of it's yours."

"You're certainly letter perfect in that speech," I says.

"And further and more," said Ella, "you remember what I told you the other day. Wile one reason we moved to New York was to see Life, the main idear was to give Kate a chance to meet real men. So every nickel we spend making ourself look good is just an investment."

"I'd rather feel good than look good," I says, "and I hate to see us spending so much money on a place to live that they won't be nothing left to live on. For three or four hundred a month you might get a joint on the Drive with a bed and two chairs, but I can't drink furniture."

"This trip wasn't planned as no spree for you," says Ella. "On the other hand, I believe Sis would stand a whole lot better show of landing the right kind of a man if the rumor was to get out that her brother-in-law stayed sober once in a wile."

"Well," I said, "I don't think my liberal attitude on the drink question affected the results of our deal in Wall Street. That investment would of turned out just as good whether I was a teetotaler or a lush."

"Listen," she says: "The next time you mention ancient history like that, I'll make a little investment in a lawyer. But what's the use of arguing? I and Kate has made up our mind to do things our own way with our own money, and to-day we're going up on the Drive with a real estate man. We won't pay no more than we can afford. All as we want is a place that's good enough and big enough for Sis to entertain her gentleman callers in it, and she certainly can't do that in this hotel."

"Well," I says, "all her gentleman callers that's been around here in the last month, she could entertain them in one bunch in a telephone booth."

"The reason she's been let alone so far," says the Mrs., "is because I won't allow her to meet the kind of men that stays at hotels. You never know who they are."

"Why not?" I said. "They've all got to register their name when they come in, which is more than you can say for people that lives in $100 apartments on Riverside Drive."

Well, my arguments went so good that for the next three days the two gals was on a home-seekers' excursion and I had to spend my time learning the eastern intercollegiate kelly pool rules up to Doyle's. I win about seventy-five dollars.

When the ladies come home the first two nights they was all wore out and singing the landlord blues, but on the third afternoon they busted in all smiles.

"We've found one," says Ella. "Six rooms, too."

"Where at?" I asked her.

"Just where we wanted it," she says. "On the Drive. And it fronts right on the Hudson."

"No!" I said. "I thought they built them all facing the other way."

"It almost seems," said Katie, "like you could reach out and touch New Jersey."

"It's what you might call a near beer apartment," I says.

"And it's almost across the street from Grant's Tomb," says Ella.

"How many rooms has he got?" I says.

"We was pretty lucky," said Ella. "The people that had it was forced to go south for the man's health. He's a kind of a cripple. And they decided to sublet it furnished. So we got a bargain."

"Come on," I says. "What price?"

"Well," she says, "they don't talk prices by the month in New York. They give you the price by the year. So it sounds a lot more than it really is. We got it for $4,000."

"Sweet patootie!" I said. "That's only half your income."

"Well, what of it?" says Ella. "It won't only be for about a year and it's in the nicest kind of a neighborhood and we can't meet nothing only the best kind of people. You know what I told you."

And she give me a sly wink.

Well, it seems like they had signed up a year's lease and paid a month's rent in advance, so what was they left for me to say? All I done was make the remark that I didn't see how we was going to come even close to a trial balance.

"Why not?" said Katie. "With our rent paid we can get along easy on $4,000 a year if we economize."

"Yes," I said. "You'll economize just like the rest of the Riverside Drivers, with a couple of servants and a car and four or five new evening dresses a month. By the end of six months the bank'll be figuring our account in marks."

"What do you mean 'our' account?" says Ella.

"But speaking about a car," said Katie, "do you suppose we could get a good one cheap?"

"Certainly," I said. "They're giving away the good ones for four double coupons."

"But I mean an inexpensive one," says Kate.

"You can't live on the River and ride in a flivver," I said. "Besides, the buses limp right by the door."

"Oh, I love the buses!" said Ella.

"Wait till you see the place," says Katie to me. "You'll go simply wild! They's a colored boy in uniform to open the door and they's two elevators."

"How high do we go?" I said.

"We're on the sixth floor," says Katie.

"I should think we could get that far in one elevator," I says.

"What was it the real estate man told us?" said Ella. "Oh, yes, he said the sixth floor was the floor everybody tried to get on."

"It's a wonder he didn't knock it," I said.

Well, we was to have immediate possession, so the next morning we checked out of this joint and swooped up on the Drive. The colored boy, who I nicknamed George, helped us up with the wardrobe. Ella had the key and inside of fifteen minutes she'd found it.

We hadn't no sooner than made our entree into our new home when I knew what ailed the previous tenant. He'd crippled himself stumbling over the furniture. The living room was big enough to stage the high hurdles, and that's what was in it, only they'd planted them every two feet apart. If a stew with the blind staggers had of walked in there in the dark, the folks on the floor below would of thought he'd knocked the head pin for a goal.

"Come across the room," said Ella, "and look at the view."

"I guess I can get there in four downs," I said, "but you better have a substitute warming up."

"Well," she says, when I'd finally fell acrost the last white chalk mark, "what do you think of it?"

"It's a damn pretty view," I says, "but I've often seen the same view from the top of a bus for a thin dime."

Well, they showed me over the whole joint and it did look O.K., but not $4,000 worth. The best thing in the place was a half full bottle of rye in the kitchen that the cripple hadn't gone south with. I did.

We got there at eleven o'clock in the morning, but at three p.m. the gals was still hanging up their Follies costumes, so I beat it out and over to Broadway and got myself a plate of pea soup. When I come back, Ella and Katie was laying down exhausted. Finally I told Ella that I was going to move back to the hotel unless they served meals in this dump, so her and Kate got up and went marketing. Well, when you move from Indiana to the Big Town, of course you can't be expected to do your own cooking, so what we had that night was from the delicatessen, and for the next four days we lived on dill pickles with dill pickles.

"Listen," I finally says: "The only reason I consented to leave the hotel was in the hopes I could get a real home cook meal once in a wile and if I don't get a real home cook meal once in a wile, I leave this dive."

"Have a little bit of patience," says Ella. "I advertised in the paper for a cook the day before we come here, the day we rented this apartment. And I offered eight dollars a week."

"How many replies did you get?" I asked her.

"Well," she said, "I haven't got none so far, but it's probably too soon to expect any."

"What did you advertise in, the world almanac?" I says.

"No, sir," she says. "I advertised in the two biggest New York papers, the ones the real estate man recommended."

"Listen," I said: "Where do you think you're at, in Niles, Michigan? If you get a cook here for eight dollars a week, it'll be a one-armed leper that hasn't yet reached her teens."

"What would you do, then?" she asked me.

"I'd write to an employment agency," I says, "and I'd tell them we'll pay good wages."

So she done that and in three days the phone rung and the agency said they had one prospect on hand and did we want her to come out and see us. So Ella said we did and out come a colleen for an interview. She asked how much we was willing to pay.

"Well," said Ella, "I'd go as high as twelve dollars. Or I'd make it fifteen if you done the washing."

Kathleen Mavourneen turned her native color.

"Well," I said, "how much do you want?"

"I'll work for ninety dollars a month," she said, only I can't get the brogue. "That's for the cookin' only. No washin'. And I would have to have a room with a bath and all day Thursdays and Sunday evenin's off."

"Nothing doing," said Ella, and the colleen started for the door.

"Wait a minute," I says. "Listen: Is that what you gals is getting in New York?"

"We're a spalpeen if we ain't," says the colleen bawn.

Well, I was desperate, so I called the wife to one side and says: "For heaven's sakes, take her on a month's trial. I'll pay the most of it with a little piece of money I picked up last week down to Doyle's. I'd rather do that than get dill pickled for a goal."

"Could you come right away?" Ella asked her.

"Not for a couple days," says Kathleen.

"It's off, then," I said. "You cook our supper to-night or go back to Greece."

"Well," she says, "I guess I could make it if I hurried."

So she went away and come back with her suitcase, and she cooked our supper that night. And Oh darlint!

Well, Beautiful Katie still had the automobile bug and it wasn't none of my business to steer her off of it and pretty near every day she would go down to the "row" and look them over. But every night she'd come home whistling a dirge.

"I guess I've seen them all," she'd say, "but they're too expensive or else they look like they wasn't."

But one time we was all coming home in a taxi from a show and come up Broadway and all of a sudden she yelled for the driver to stop.

"That's a new one in that window," she says, "and one I never see before."

Well, the dive was closed at the time and we couldn't get in, but she insisted on going down there the first thing in the morning and I and Ella must go along. The car was a brand new model Bam Eight.

"How much?" I asked him.

"Four thousand," he says.

"When could I get one?" says Katie.

"I don't know," said the salesman.

"What do you mean?" I asked him. "Haven't they made none of them?"

"I don't know," says the salesman. "This is the only one we got."

"Has anybody ever rode in one?" I says.

"I don't know," said the guy.

So I asked him what made it worth four thousand.

"Well," he says, "what made this lady want one?"

"I don't know," I said.

"Could I have this one that's on the floor?" says Katie.

"I don't know," said the salesman.

"Well, when do you think I could get one?" says Katie.

"We can't promise no deliveries," says the salesman.

Well, that kind of fretted me, so I asked him if they wasn't a salesman we could talk to.

"You're talking to one," he said.

"Yes, I know," said I. "But I used to be a kind of a salesman myself, and when I was trying to sell things, I didn't try and not sell them."

"Yes," he says, "but you wasn't selling automobiles in New York in 1920. Listen," he says: "I'll be frank with you. We got the New York agency for this car and was glad to get it because it sells for four thousand and anything that sells that high, why the people will eat up, even if it's a pearl-handle ketchup bottle. If we ever do happen to get a consignment of these cars, they'll sell like oil stock. The last word we got from the factory was that they'd send us three cars next September. So that means we'll get two cars a year from next October and if we can spare either of them, you can have one."

So then he begin to yawn and I said, "Come on, girls," and we got a taxi and beat it home. And I wouldn't of said nothing about it, only if Katie had of been able to buy her Bam, what come off might of never came off.

It wasn't only two nights later when Ella come in from shopping all excited. "Well," she said, "talk about experiences! I just had a ride home and it wasn't in a street car and it wasn't in a taxi and it wasn't on the Subway and it wasn't on a bus."

"Let's play charades," said I.

"Tell us, Sis," says Katie.

"Well," said the wife, "I was down on Fifth Avenue, waiting for a bus, and all of a sudden a big limousine drew up to the curb with a livery chauffeur, and a man got out of the back seat and took off his hat and asked if he couldn't see me home. And of course I didn't pay no attention to him."

"Of course not," I said.

"But," says Ella, "he says, 'Don't take no offense. I think we're next door neighbors. Don't you live acrost the hall on the sixth floor of the Lucius?' So of course I had to tell him I did."

"Of course," I said.

"And then he said," says Ella, "'Is that your sister living with you?' 'Yes,' I said, 'she lives with my husband and I.' 'Well,' he says, 'if you'll get in and let me take you home, I'll tell you what a beautiful girl I think she is.' So I seen then that he was all right, so I got in and come home with him. And honestly, Sis, he's just wild about you!"

"What is he like?" says Katie.

"He's stunning," says the wife. "Tall and wears dandy clothes and got a cute mustache that turns up."

"How old?" says Kate, and the Mrs. kind of stalled.

"Well," she said, "he's the kind of a man that you can't tell how old they are, but he's not old. I'd say he was, well, maybe he's not even that old."

"What's his name?" asked Kate.

"Trumbull," said the Mrs. "He said he was keeping bachelor quarters, but I don't know if he's really a bachelor or a widower. Anyway, he's a dandy fella and must have lots of money. Just imagine living alone in one of these apartments!"

"Imagine living in one of them whether you're a bachelor or a Mormon," I says.

"Who said he lived alone?" asked Katie.

"He did," says the Mrs. "He told me that him and his servants had the whole apartment to themselves. And that's what makes it so nice, because he's asked the three of us over there to dinner tomorrow night."

"What makes it so nice?" I asked her.

"Because it does," said Ella, and you can't ever beat an argument like that.

So the next night the two girls donned their undress uniforms and made me put on the oysters and horse radish and we went acrost the hall to meet our hero. The door was opened by a rug peddler and he showed us into a twin brother to our own living room, only you could get around it without being Houdini.

"Mr. Trumbull will be right out," said Omar.

The ladies was shaking like an aspirin leaf, but in a few minutes, in come mine host. However old Ella had thought he wasn't, she was wrong. He'd seen baseball when the second bounce was out. If he'd of started his career as a barber in Washington, he'd of tried to wish a face massage on Zachary

Taylor. The only thing young about him was his teeth and his clothes. His dinner suit made me feel like I was walking along the station platform at Toledo, looking for hot boxes.

"Ah, here you are!" he says. "It's mighty nice of you to be neighborly. And so this is the young sister. Well," he says to me, "you had your choice, and as far as I can see, it was heads you win and tails you win. You're lucky."

So when he'd spread all the salve, he rung the bell and in come Allah with cocktails. I don't know what was in them, but when Ella and Katie had had two apiece, they both begin to trill.

Finally we was called in to dinner and every other course was hootch. After the solid and liquid diet, he turned on the steam piano and we all danced. I had one with Beautiful Katie and the rest of them was with my wife, or, as I have nicknamed them, quarrels. Well, the steam run out of three of us at the same time, the piano inclusive, and Ella sat down in a chair that was made for Eddie Foy's family and said how comfortable it was.

"Yes," says Methuselah, "that's my favorite chair. And I bet you wouldn't believe me if I told you how much it cost."

"Oh, I'd like to know," says Ella.

"Two hundred dollars," says mine host.

"Do you still feel comfortable?" I asked her.

"Speaking about furniture," said the old bird, "I've got a few bits that I'm proud of. Would you like to take a look at them?"

So the gals said they would and we had to go through the entire apartment, looking at bits. The best bits I seen was tastefully wrapped up in kegs and cases. It seemed like every time he opened a drawer, a cork popped up. He was a hundred per cent, proofer than the governor of New Jersey. But he was giving us a lecture on the furniture itself, not the polish.

"I picked up this dining room suit for eighteen hundred," he says.

"Do you mean the one you've got on?" I asked him, and the gals give me a dirty look.

"And this rug," he says, stomping on an old rag carpet. "How much do you suppose that cost?"

It was my first guess, so I said fifty dollars.

"That's a laugh," he said. "I paid two thousand for that rug."

"The guy that sold it had the laugh," I says.

Finally he steered us into his bedroom.

"Do you see that bed?" he says. "That's Marie Antoinette's bed. Just a cool thousand."

"What time does she usually get in?" I asked him.

"Here's my hobby," he said, opening up a closet, "dressing gowns and bathrobes."

Well, they was at least a dozen of them hanging on hangers. They was all colors of the rainbow including the Scandinavian. He dragged one down that was redder than Ella's and Katie's cheeks.

"This is my favorite bathrobe," he said. "It's Rose D. Barry."

So I asked him if he had all his household goods and garments named after some dame.

"This bathrobe cost me an even two hundred," he says.

"I always take baths bare," I said. "It's a whole lot cheaper."

"Let's go back in the living room," says Katie.

"Come on," said Ella, tugging me by the sleeve.

"Wait a minute," I says to her. "I don't know how much he paid for his toothbrush."

Well, when we got back in the living room, the two gals acted kind of drowsy and snuggled up together on the davenport and I and the old bird was left to ourself.

"Here's another thing I didn't show you," he says, and pulls a pair of African golf balls out of a drawer in his desk. "These dice is real ivory and they cost me twelve and a half berries."

"You mean up to now," I said.

"All right," he said. "We'll make it a twenty-five dollar limit."

Well, I didn't have no business in a game with him, but you know how a guy gets sometimes. So he took them first and rolled a four.

"Listen," I says: "Do you know how many times Willard set down in the first round?"

And sure enough he sevened.

"Now solid ivory dice," I said, "how many days in the week?"

So out come a natural. And as sure as I'm setting here, I made four straight passes with the whole roll riding each time and with all that wad parked on the two thousand dollar rug, I shot a five and a three. "Ivory," I said, "we was invited here to-night, so don't make me pay for the entertainment. Show me eighter from Decatur."

And the lady from Decatur showed.

Just then they was a stir on the davenport, and Ella woke up long enough to make the remark that we ought to go home. It was the first time she ever said it in the right place.

"Oh," I says, "I've got to give Mr. Trumbull a chance to get even."

But I wasn't in earnest.

"Don't bother about that," said Old Noah. "You can accommodate me some other time."

"You're certainly a sport," I says.

"And thanks for a wonderful time," said Ella. "I hope we'll see you again soon."

"Soon is to-morrow night," said mine host. "I'm going to take you all up the river to a place I know."

"Well," I says to Katie, when we was acrost the hall and the door shut, "how do you like him?"

"Oh, shut up!" says Katie.

So the next night he come over and rung our bell and said Ritchey was waiting with the car and would we come down when we was ready. Well, the gals had only had all day to prepare for the trip, so in another half hour they had their wraps on and we went downstairs. They wasn't nothing in front but a Rools-Royce with a livery chauffeur that looked like he'd been put there by a rubber stamp.

"What a stunning driver!" said Katie when we'd parked ourself in the back seat.

"Ritchey?" says mine host. "He is a nice looking boy, but better than that, he's a boy I can trust."

Well, anyway, the boy he could trust took us out to a joint called the Indian Inn where you wouldn't of never knew they was an eighteenth amendment only that the proprietor was asking twenty berries a quart for stuff that used to cost four. But that didn't seem to bother Methuselah and he ordered two of them. Not only that but he got us a table so close to the orchestra that the cornet player thought we was his mute.

"Now, what'll we eat?" he says.

So I looked at the program and the first item I seen was "Guinea Hen, $4.50."

"That's what Katie'll want," I says to myself, and sure enough that's what she got.

Well, we eat and then we danced and we danced and we danced, and finally along about eleven I and Ella was out on the floor pretending like we was enjoying ourself, and we happened to look over to the table and there was Katie and Trumbull setting one out and to look at either you could tell that something was wrong.

"Dance the next one with her," says Ella, "and find out what's the matter."

So I danced the next one with Katie and asked her.

"He squeezed my hand," she says. "I don't like him."

"Well," said I, "if you'd of ordered guinea hen on me I wouldn't of stopped at your hand. I'd of went at your throat."

"I've got a headache," she says. "Take me out to the car."

So they was nothing to it but I had to take her out to the car and come back and tell Ella and Trumbull that she wasn't feeling any too good and wanted to go home.

"She don't like me," says the old guy. "That's the whole trouble."

"Give her time," says Ella. "Remember she's just a kid."

"Yes, but what a kid!" he says.

So then he paid the cheek without no competition and we went out and dumb in the big limmie. Katie was pretending like she was asleep and neither Ella or Trumbull acted like they wanted to talk, so the conversation on the way home was mostly one-sided, with me in the title role. Katie went in the apartment without even thanking mine host for the guinea hen, but he kept Ella and I outside long enough to say that Ritchey and the car was at our service any time we wanted them.

So Ella told her that the next noon at breakfast. "And you'd ought to be ashamed of yourself," says Ella, "for treating a man like that like that."

"He's too fresh," says Katie.

"Well," said Ella, "if he was a little younger, you wouldn't mind him being fresh."

"No," said Katie, "if he was fresh, I wouldn't care if he was fresh. But what's the number of the garage?"

And she didn't lose no time taking advantage of the old bird. That same afternoon it seemed she had to go shopping and the bus wasn't good enough no more. She was out in Trumbull's limmie from two o'clock till pretty near seven. The old guy himself come to our place long about five and wanted to know if we knew where she was at. "I haven't no idear," said Ella. "I expected her home long ago. Did you want to use the car?"

"What's the difference," I said, "if he wanted to use the car or not? He's only the owner."

"Well," says Trumbull, "when I make an offer I mean it, and that little girl is welcome to use my machine whenever she feels like it."

So Ella asked him to stay to dinner and he said he would if we'd allow him to bring in some of his hootch, and of course I kicked on that proposition, but he insisted. And when Katie finally did get home, we was all feeling good and so was she and you'd never of thought they'd been any bad feelings the night before.

Trumbull asked her what she'd been buying.

"Nothing," she says. "I was looking at dresses, but they want too much money."

"You don't need no dresses," he says.

"No, of course not," said Katie. "But lots of girls is wearing them."

"Where did you go?" said Ella.

"I forget," says Katie. "What do you say if we play cards?"

So we played rummy till we was all blear-eyed and the old guy left, saying we'd all go somewheres next day. After he'd gone Ella begin to talk serious.

"Sis," she says, "here's the chance of a lifetime. Mr. Trumbull's head over heels in love with you and all as you have to do is encourage him a little. Can't you try and like him?"

"They's nobody I have more respect for," said Katie, "unless it's George Washington."

And then she give a funny laugh and run off to bed.

"I can't understand Sis no more," said Ella, when we was alone.

"Why not?" I asked her.

"Why, look at this opportunity staring her in the face," says the Mrs.

"Listen," I said: "The first time I stared you in the face, was you thinking about opportunity?"

Well, to make a short story out of it, I was the only one up in the house the next morning when Kathleen said we had a caller. It was the old boy.

"I'm sorry to be so early," he says, "but I just got a telegram and it means I got to run down to Washington for a few days. And I wanted to tell you that wile I'm gone Ritchey and the car is at your service."

So I thanked him and he said good-by and give his regards to the Mrs. and especially Katie, so when they got up I told them about it and I never seen a piece of bad news received so calm as Katie took it.

"But now he's gone," I said at the breakfast table, "why not the three of us run out to Bridgeport and call on the Wilmots?"

They're cousins of mine.

"Oh, fine!" said Ella.

"Wait a minute," says Katie. "I made a kind of an engagement with a dressmaker for to-day."

Well, as I say, to make a short story out of it, it seems like she'd made engagements with the dressmaker every day, but they wasn't no dresses ever come home.

In about a week Trumbull come back from Washington and the first thing he done was look us up and we had him in to dinner and I don't remember how the conversation started, but all of a sudden we was on the subject of his driver, Ritchey.

"A great boy," says Trumbull, "and a boy you can trust. If I didn't like him for nothing else, I'd like him for how he treats his family."

"What family?" says Kate.

"Why," says Trumbull, "his own family: his wife and two kids."

"My heavens!" says Katie, and kind of fell in a swoon.

So it seems like we didn't want to live there no more and we moved back to the Baldwin, having sublet the place on the Drive for three thousand a year.

So from then on, we was paying a thousand per annum for an apartment we didn't live in two weeks. But as I told the gals, we was getting pretty near as much for our money as the people that rented New York apartments and lived in them, too.

III

LADY PERKINS

Along the first week in May they was a couple hot days, and Katie can't stand the heat. Or the cold, or the medium. Anyway, when it's hot she always says: "I'm simply stifling." And when it's cold: "I'm simply frozen." And when it ain't neither one: "I wished the weather would do one thing another." I don't s'pose she knows what she's saying when she says any one of them things, but she's one of these here gals that can't bear to see a conversation die out and thinks it's her place to come through with a wise crack whenever they's a vacuum.

So during this hot spell we was having dinner with a bird named Gene Buck that knowed New York like a book, only he hadn't never read a book, and Katie made the remark that she was simply stifling.

"If you think this is hot," says our friend, "just wait till the summer comes. The Old Town certainly steams up in the Old Summer Time."

So Kate asked him how people could stand it.

"They don't," he says. "All the ones that's got a piece of change ducks out somewheres where they can get the air."

"Where do they go?" Katie asked him.

"Well," he says, "the most of my pals goes to Newport or Maine or up in the Adirondacks. But of course them places is out of most people's reach. If I was you folks I'd go over on Long Island somewheres and either take a cottage or live in one of them good hotels."

"Where, for instance?" says my Mrs.

"Well," he said, "some people takes cottages, but the rents is something fierce, and besides, the desirable ones is probably all eat up by this time. But they's plenty good hotels where you get good service and swell meals and meet good people; they won't take in no riffraff. And they give you a pretty fair rate if they know you're going to make a stay."

So Ella asked him if they was any special one he could recommend.

"Let's think a minute," he says.

"Let's not strain ourself," I said.

"Don't get cute!" said the Mrs. "We want to get some real information and Mr. Buck can give it to us."

"How much would you be willing to pay?" said Buck.

It was Ella's turn to make a wise crack.

"Not no more than we have to," she says.

"I and my sister has got about eight thousand dollars per annum between us," said Katie, "though a thousand of it has got to go this year to a man that cheated us up on Riverside Drive.

"It was about a lease. But papa left us pretty well off; over a hundred and fifty thousand dollars."

"Don't be so secret with Mr. Buck," I says. "We've knew him pretty near a week now. Tell him about them four-dollar stockings you bought over on Fifth Avenue and the first time you put them on they got as many runs as George Sisler."

"Well," said Buck, "I don't think you'd have no trouble getting comfortable rooms in a good hotel on seven thousand dollars. If I was you I'd try the Hotel Decker. It's owned by a man named Decker."

"Why don't he call it the Griffith!" I says.

"It's located at Tracy Estates," says Buck. "That's one of the garden spots of Long Island. It's a great big place, right up to the minute, and they give you everything the best. And they's three good golf courses within a mile of the hotel."

The gals told him they didn't play no golf.

"You don't know what you've missed," he says.

"Well," I said, "I played a game once myself and missed a whole lot."

"Do they have dances?" asked Kate.

"Plenty of them," says Buck, "and the guests is the nicest people you'd want to meet. Besides all that, the meals is included in the rates, and they certainly set a nasty table."

"I think it sounds grand," said the Mrs. "How do you get there?"

"Go over to the Pennsylvania Station," says Buck, "and take the Long Island Railroad to Jamaica. Then you change to the Haverton branch. It don't only take a half hour altogether,"

"Let's go over to-morrow morning and see can we get rooms," said Katie.

So Ella asked how that suited me.

"Go just as early as you want to," I says. "I got a date to run down to the Aquarium and see the rest of the fish."

"You won't make no mistake stopping at the Decker," says Buck.

So the gals thanked him and I paid the check so as he would have more to spend when he joined his pals up to Newport.

Well, when Ella and Kate come back the next afternoon, I could see without them telling me that it was all settled. They was both grinning like they always do when they've pulled something nutty.

"It's a good thing we met Mr. Buck," said the Mrs., "or we mightn't never of heard of this place. It's simply wonderful. A double room with a bath for you and I and a room with a bath for Katie. The meals is throwed in, and we can have it all summer."

"How much?" I asked her.

"Two hundred a week," she said. "But you must remember that's for all three of us and we get our meals free."

"And I s'pose they also furnish knobs for the bedroom doors," says I.

"We was awful lucky," said the wife. "These was the last two rooms they had, and they wouldn't of had those only the lady that had engaged them canceled her reservation."

"I wished I'd met her when I was single," I says.

"So do I," says Ella.

"But listen," I said. "Do you know what two hundred a week amounts to? It amounts to over ten thousand a year, and our income is seven thousand."

"Yes," says Katie, "but we aren't only going to be there twenty weeks, and that's only four thousand."

"Yes," I said, "and that leaves us three thousand for the other thirty-two weeks, to pay for board and room and clothes and show tickets and a permanent wave every other day."

"You forget," said Kate, "that we still got our principal, which we can spend some of it and not miss it."

"And you also forget," said the Mrs., "that the money belongs to Sis and I, not you."

"I've got a sweet chance of forgetting that," I said. "It's hammered into me three times a day. I hear about it pretty near as often as I hear that one of you's lost their new silk bag."

"Well, anyway," says Ella, "it's all fixed up and we move out there early tomorrow morning, so you'll have to do your packing to-night."

I'm not liable to celebrate the anniversary of the next day's trip. Besides the trunks, the gals had a suitcase and a grip apiece and I had a suitcase. So that give me five pieces of baggage to wrestle, because of course the gals had to carry their parasol in one hand and their wrist watch in the other. A redcap helped load us on over to the station, but oh you change at Jamaica! And when we got to Tracy Estates we seen that the hotel wasn't only a couple of blocks away, so the ladies said we might as well walk and save taxi fare.

I don't know how I covered them two blocks, but I do know that when I reeled into the Decker my hands and arms was paralyzed and Ella had to do the registering.

Was you ever out there? Well, I s'pose it's what you might call a family hotel, and a good many of the guests belongs to the cay-nine family. A few of the couples that can't afford dogs has got children, and you're always tripping over one or the other. They's a dining room for the grown-ups and another for the kids, wile the dogs and their nurses eats in the grillroom a la carte. One part of the joint is bachelor quarters. It's located right next to the dogs' dormitories, and they's a good deal of rivalry between the dogs and the souses to see who can make the most noise nights. They's also a ballroom and a couple card rooms and a kind of a summer parlor where the folks sets round in the evening and listen to a three-piece orchestra that don't know they's been any music wrote since Poets and Peasants. The men get up about eight o'clock and go down to New York to Business. They don't never go to work. About nine the women begins limping downstairs and either goes to call on their dogs or take them for a walk in the front yard. This is a great big yard with a whole lot of benches strewed round it, but you can't set on them in the daytime because the women or the nurses uses them for a place to read to the dogs or kids, and in the evenings you would have to share them with the waitresses, which you have already had enough of them during the day.

When the women has prepared themselves for the long day's grind with a four-course breakfast, they set round on the front porch and discuss the big questions of the hour, like for instance the last trunk murder or whether an Airedale is more loving than a Golden Bantam. Once in a wile one of them cracks that it looks like they was bound to be a panic pretty soon and a big drop in prices, and so forth. This shows they're broad-minded and are giving a good deal of thought to up-to-date topics. Every so often one of them'll say: "The present situation can't keep up." The hell it can't!

By one o'clock their appetites is whetted so keen from brain exercise that they make a bum out of a plate of soup and an order of Long Island duckling, which they figure is caught fresh every day, and they wind up with salad and apple pie à la mode and a stein of coffee. Then they totter up to their rooms to sleep it off before Dear gets home from Business.

Saturday nights everybody puts on their evening clothes like something was going to happen. But it don't. Sunday mornings the husbands and bachelors gets up earlier than usual to go to their real business, which is golf. The womenfolks are in full possession of the hotel till Sunday night supper and wives and husbands don't see one another all day long, but it don't seem as long as if they did. Most of them's approaching their golden-wedding jubilee and haven't nothing more to say to each other that you could call a novelty. The husband may make the remark, Sunday night, that he would of broke one hundred and twenty in the afternoon round if the caddy hadn't of handed him a spoon when he asked for a nut pick, and the wife'll probably reply that she's got to go in Town some day soon and see a chiropodist. The rest of the Sabbath evening is spent in bridge or listening to the latest song hit from The Bohemian Girl.

The hotel's got all the modern conveniences like artificial light and a stopper in the bathtubs. They even got a barber and a valet, but you can't get a shave wile he's pressing your clothes, so it's pretty near impossible for a man to look their best at the same time.

Well, the second day we was there I bought me a deck of cards and got so good at solitary that pretty soon I could play fifty games between breakfast and lunch and a hundred from then till suppertime. During the first week Ella and Kate got on friendly terms with over a half dozen people—the head waiter, our waitress, some of the clerks and the manager and the two telephone gals. It wasn't from lack of trying that they didn't meet even more people. Every day one or the other of them would try and swap a little small talk with one of the other squatters, but it generally always wound up as a short monologue.

Ella said to me one day, she says: "I don't know if we can stick it out here or not. Every hotel I was ever at before, it was easy enough to make a lot of friends, but you could stick a bottle of cream alongside one of these people and it'd stay sweet a week. Unless they looked at it. I'm sick of talking to you and Sis and the hired help, and Kate's so lonesome that she cries herself to sleep nights."

Well, if I'd of only had sense enough to insist on staying we'd of probably packed up and took the next train to Town. But instead of that I said: "What's to prevent us from going back to New York?"

"Don't be silly!" says the Mrs. "We come out here to spend the summer and here is where we're going to spend the summer."

"All right," I says, "and by September I'll be all set to write a book on one-handed card games."

"You'd think," says Ella, "that some of these women was titled royalties the way they snap at you when you try and be friends with them. But they's only one in the bunch that's got any handle to her name; that's Lady Perkins."

I asked her which one was that.

"You know," says Ella. "I pointed her out to you in the dining room. She's a nice-looking woman, about thirty-five, that sets near our table and walks with a cane."

"If she eats like some of the rest of them," I says, "she's lucky they don't have to w'eel her."

"She's English," says Ella. "They just come over and her husband's in Texas on some business and left her here. She's the one that's got that dog."

"That dog!" I said. "You might just as well tell me she's the one that don't play the mouth organ. They've all got a dog."

"She's got two," said the wife. "But the one I meant is that big German police dog that I'm scared to death of him. Haven't you saw her out walking with him and the little chow?"

"Yes," I said, "if that's what it is. I always wondered what the boys in the Army was talking about when they said they eat chow."

"They probably meant chowchow," says the Mrs. "They wouldn't of had these kind of chows, because in the first place, who would eat a dog, and besides these kind costs too much."

"Well," I says, "I'm not interested in the price of chows, but if you want to get acquainted with Lady Perkins, why I can probably fix it for you."

"Yes, you'll fix it!" said Ella. "I'm begining to think that if we'd of put you in storage for the summer the folks round here wouldn't shy away from us like we was leopards that had broke out of a pesthouse. I wished you would try and dress up once in a wile and not always look like you was just going to do the chores. Then maybe I and Sis might get somewheres."

Well, of course when I told her I could probably fix it up with Lady Perkins, I didn't mean nothing. But it wasn't only the next morning when I started making good. I was up and dressed and downstairs about half past eight, and as the gals wasn't ready for their breakfast yet I went out on the porch and set down. They wasn't nobody else there, but pretty soon I seen Lady Perkins come up the path with her two whelps. "When she got to the porch steps their nurse popped out of the servants' quarters and took them round to the grillroom for their breakfast. I s'pose the big one ordered sauerkraut and kalter Aufschnitt, wile the chow had tea and eggs fo yung. Anyway, the Perkins dame come up on the porch and flopped into the chair next to mine.

In a few minutes Ed Wurz, the manager of the hotel, showed, with a bag of golf instruments and a trick suit. He spotted me and asked me if I didn't want to go along with him and play.

"No," I said. "I only played once in my life."

"That don't make no difference," he says. "I'm a bum myself. I just play shinny, you might say."

"Well," I says, "I can't anyway, on account of my dogs. They been giving me a lot of trouble."

Of course I was referring to my feet, but he hadn't no sooner than went on his way when Lady Perkins swung round on me and says: "I didn't know you had dogs. Where do you keep them?"

At first I was going to tell her "In my shoes," but I thought I might as well enjoy myself, so I said: "They're in the dog hospital over to Haverton."

"What ails them?" she asked me.

Well, I didn't know nothing about caynine diseases outside of hydrophobia, which don't come till August, so I had to make one up.

"They got blanny," I told her.

"Blanny!" she says. "I never heard of it before."

"No," I said. "It hasn't only been discovered in this country just this year. It got carried up here from Peru some way another."

"Oh, it's contagious, then!" says Lady Perkins.

"Worse than measles or lockjaw," says I. "You take a dog that's been in the same house with a dog that's got blanny, and it's a miracle if they don't all get it."

She asked me if I'd had my dogs in the hotel.

"Only one day," I says, "the first day we come, about a week ago. As soon as I seen what was the matter with them, I took them over to Haverton in a sanitary truck."

"Was they mingling with the other dogs here?" she says.

"Just that one day," I said.

"Heavens!" said Lady Perkins. "And what's the symptoms?"

"Well," I said, "first you'll notice that they keep their tongue stuck out a lot and they're hungry a good deal of the time, and finally they show up with a rash."

"Then what happens?" she says. "Well," said I, "unless they get the best of treatment, they kind of dismember."

Then she asked me how long it took for the symptoms to show after a dog had been exposed. I told her any time between a week and four months.

"My dogs has been awful hungry lately," she says, "and they most always keeps their tongue stuck out. But they haven't no rash."

"You're all right, then," I says. "If you give them treatments before the rash shows up, they's no danger."

"What's the treatment?" she asked me.

"You rub the back of their neck with some kind of dope," I told her. "I forget what it is, but if you say the word, I can get you a bottle of it when I go over to the hospital this afternoon."

"I'd be ever so much obliged," she says, "and I hope you'll find your dear ones a whole lot better."

"Dear ones is right," I said. "They cost a pile of jack, and the bird I bought them off of told me I should ought to get them insured, but I didn't. So if anything happens to them now, I'm just that much out."

Next she asked me what kind of dogs they was.

"Well," I said, "you might maybe never of heard of them, as they don't breed them nowheres only way down in Dakota. They call them yaphounds—I don't know why; maybe on account of the noise they make. But they're certainly a grand-looking dog and they bring a big price."

She set there a wile longer and then got up and went inside, probably to the nursery to look for signs of rash.

Of course I didn't tell the Mrs. and Kate nothing about this incidence. They wouldn't of believed it if I had of, and besides, it would be a knock-out if things broke right and Lady Perkins come up and spoke to me wile they was present, which is just what happened.

During the afternoon I strolled over to the drug store and got me an empty pint bottle. I took it up in the room and filled it with water and shaving soap. Then I laid low till evening, so as Perk would think I had went to Haverton.

I and Ella and Kate breezed in the dining room kind of late and we hadn't no more than ordered when I seen the Lady get up and start out. She had to pass right past us, and when I looked at her and smiled she stopped.

"Well," she said, "how's your dogs?"

I got up from the table.

"A whole lot better, thank you," says I, and then I done the honors. "Lady Perkins," I said, "meet the wife and sister-in-law."

The two gals staggered from their chairs, both pop-eyed. Lady Perkins bowed to them and told them to set down. If she hadn't the floor would of bounced up and hit them in the chin.

"I got a bottle for you," I said. "I left it upstairs and I'll fetch it down after supper."

"I'll be in the red card room," says Perk, and away she went.

I wished you could of see the two gals. They couldn't talk for a minute, for the first time in their life. They just set there with their mouth open like a baby blackbird. Then they both broke out with a rash of questions that come so fast I couldn't understand none of them, but the general idear was, What the hell!

"They's no mystery about it," I said. "Lady Perkins was setting out on the porch this morning and you two was late getting down to breakfast, so I took a walk, and when I come back she noticed that I kind of limped and asked me what ailed my feet. I told her they always swoll up in warm weather and she said she was troubled the same way and did I know any medicine that shrank them. So I told her I had a preparation and would bring her a bottle of it."

"But," says Kate, "I can't understand a woman like she speaking to a man she don't know."

"She's been eying me all week," I said. "I guess she didn't have the nerve to break the ice up to this morning; then she got desperate."

"She must of," said Ella.

"I wished," said Kate, "that when you introduce me to people you'd give them my name."

"I'm sorry," I said, "but I couldn't recall it for a minute, though your face is familiar."

"But listen," says the wife. "What ails your dogs is a corn. You haven't got no swelled feet and you haven't got no medicine for them."

"Well," I says, "what I give her won't hurt her. It's just a bottle of soap and water that I mixed up, and pretty near everybody uses that once in a wile without no bad after effects."

Now, the whole three of us had been eating pretty good ever since we'd came to the Decker. After living à la carte at Big Town prices for six months, the American plan was sweet patootie. But this night the gals not only skrimped themselves but they was in such a hurry for me to get through that my molars didn't hardly have time to identify what all was scampering past them. Ella finally got so nervous that I had to take off the feed bag without dipping my bill into the stewed rhubarb.

"Lady Perkins will get tired waiting for you," she says. "And besides, she won't want us horning in there and interrupting them after their game's started."

"Us!" said I. "How many do you think it's going to take to carry this bottle?"

"You don't mean to say we can't go with you!" said Kate.

"You certainly can't," I says. "I and the nobility won't have our little romance knocked for a gool by a couple of country gals that can't get on speaking terms with nobody but the chambermaid."

"But they'll be other people there," says Kate. "She can't play cards alone."

"Who told you she was going to play cards?" I says. "She picked the red card room because we ain't liable to be interrupted there. As for playing cards alone, what else have I done all week?

But when I get there she won't have to play solitary. It'll be two-handed hearts; where if you was to crowd in, it couldn't be nothing but rummy."

Well, they finally dragged me from the table, and the gals took a seat in the lobby wile I went upstairs after the medicine. But I hadn't no sooner than got a hold of the bottle when Ella come in the room.

"Listen," she says. "They's a catch in this somewheres. You needn't to try and tell me that a woman like Lady Perkins is trying to start a flirtation with a yahoo. Let's hear what really come off."

"I already told you," I said. "The woman's nuts over me and you should ought to be the last one to find fault with her judgment."

Ella didn't speak for a wile. Then she says: "Well, if you're going to forget your marriage vows and flirt with an old hag like she, I guess two can play at that little game. They's several men round this hotel that I like their looks and all as they need is a little encouragement."

"More than a little, I guess," says I, "or else they'd of already been satisfied with what you and Kate has give them. They can't neither one of you pretend that you been fighting on the defense all week, and the reason you haven't copped nobody is because this place is a hotel, not a home for the blind."

I wrapped a piece of newspaper round the bottle and started for the door. But all of a sudden I heard snuffles and stopped.

"Look here," I said. "I been kidding you. They's no need for you to get sore and turn on the tear ducks. I'll tell you how this thing happened if you think you can see a joke."

So I give her the truth, and afterwards I says: "They'll be plenty of time for you and Kate to get acquainted with the dame, but I don't want you tagging in there with me to-night. She'd think we was too cordial. To-morrow morning, if you can manage to get up, we'll all three of us go out on the porch and lay for her when she brings the whelps back from their hike. She's sure to stop and inquire about my kennel. And don't forget, wile she's talking, that we got a couple of yaphounds that's suffering from blanny, and if she asks any questions let me do the answering, as I can think a lot quicker. You better tell Kate the secret, too, before she messes everything up, according to custom."

Then I and the Mrs. come downstairs and her and Katie went out to listen to the music wile I beat it to the red card room. I give Perkie the bottle of rash poison and she thanked me and said she would have the dogs' governess slap some of it onto them in the morning. She was playing bridge w'ist with another gal and two dudes. To look at their faces they wasn't playing for just pins. I had sense enough to not talk, but I stood there watching them a few minutes. Between hands Perk introduced me to the rest of the party. She had to ask my name first. The other skirt at the table was a Mrs. Snell and one of the dudes was a Doctor Platt. I didn't get the name of Lady Perkins' partner.

"Mr. Finch," says Perk, "is also a dog fancier. But his dogs is sick with a disease called blanny and he's got them over to the dog hospital at Haverton."

"What kind of dogs?" asked Platt.

"I never heard of the breed before," says Perk. "They're yaphounds."

"They raise them in South Dakota," I says.

Platt gives me a funny look and said: "I been in South Dakota several times and I never heard of a yaphound neither; or I never heard of a disease named blanny."

"I s'pose not," says I. "You ain't the only old-fashioned doctor that left themself go to seed when they got out of school. I bet you won't admit they's such a thing as appendicitis."

Well, this got a laugh from Lady Perkins and the other dude, but it didn't go very big with Doc or Mrs. Snell. Wile Doc was trying to figure out a come-back I said I must go and look after my womenfolks. So I told the party I was glad to of met them and walked out.

I found Ella and Katie in the summer parlor, and they wasn't alone. A nice looking young fella named Codd was setting alongside of them, and after we was introduced Ella leaned over and w'ispered to me that he was Bob Codd, the famous aviator. It come out that he had invented some new kind of an aeroplane and had came to demonstrate it to the Williams Company. The company—Palmer Williams and his brother, you know—they've got their flying field a couple miles from the hotel. Well, a guy with nerve enough to go up in one of them things certainly ain't going to hesitate about speaking to a strange gal when he likes their looks. So this Codd baby had give himself an introduction to my Mrs. and Kate, and I guess they hadn't sprained an ankle running away from him.

Of course Ella wanted to know how I'd came out with Lady Perkins. I told her that we hadn't had much chance to talk because she was in a bridge game with three other people, but I'd met them and they'd all seemed to fall for me strong. Ella wanted to know who they was and I told her their names, all but the one I didn't get. She squealed when I mentioned Mrs. Snell.

"Did you hear that, Sis?" she says to Kate. "Tom's met Mrs. Snell. That's the woman, you know, that wears them funny clothes and has the two dogs."

"You're describing every woman in the hotel," I said.

"But this is *the* Mrs. Snell," said the wife. "Her husband's the sugar man and she's the daughter of George Henkel, the banker. They say she's a wonderful bridge player and don't never play only for great big stakes. I'm wild to meet her."

"Yes," I said, "if they's one person you should ought to meet, it's a wonderful bridge player that plays for great big stakes, especially when our expenses is making a bum out of our income and you don't know a grand slam from no dice."

"I don't expect to gamble with her," says Ella. "But she's just the kind of people we want to know."

Well, the four of us set there and talked about this and that, and Codd said he hadn't had time to get his machine put together yet, but when he had her fixed and tested her a few times he would take me up for a ride.

"You got the wrong number," I says. "I don't feel flighty."

"Oh, I'd just love it!" said Kate.

"Well," says Codd, "you ain't barred. But I don't want to have no passengers along till I'm sure she's working O.K."

When I and Ella was upstairs she said that Codd had told them he expected to sell his invention to the Williamses for a cold million. And he had took a big fancy to Kate.

"Well," I said, "they say that the reckless aviators makes the best ones, so if him and Kate gets married he'll be better than ever. He won't give a damn after that."

"You're always saying something nasty about Sis," said the Mrs.; "but I know you just talk to hear yourself talk. If I thought you meant it I'd walk out on you."

"I'd hate to lose you," I says, "but if you took her along I wouldn't write it down as a total loss."

The following morning I and the two gals was down on the porch bright and early and in a few minutes, sure enough, along came Lady Perkins, bringing the menagerie back from the parade. She turned them over to the nurse and joined us. She said that Martha, the nurse, had used the rash poison and it had made a kind of a lather on the dogs' necks and she didn't know whether to wash it off or not, but it had dried up in the sun. She asked me how many times a day the dope should ought to be put on, and I told her before every meal and at bedtime.

"But," I says, "it's best to not take the dogs right out in the sun where the lather'll dry. The blanny germ can't live in that kind of lather, so the longer it stays moist, why, so much the better."

Then she asked me was I going to Haverton to see my pets that day and I said yes, and she said she hoped I'd find them much improved. Then Ella cut in and said she understood that Lady Perkins was very fond of bridge.

"Yes, I am," says Perk. "Do you people play?"

"No, we don't," says Ella, "but we'd like to learn."

"It takes a long wile to learn to play good," said Perk. "But I do wished they was another real player in the hotel so as we wouldn't have to take Doctor Platt in. He knows the game, but he don't know enough to keep still. I don't mind people talking wile the cards is being dealt, but once the hands is picked up they ought to be absolute silence. Last night I lost about three hundred and seventy dollars just because he talked at the wrong time."

"Three hundred and seventy dollars!" said Kate. "My, you must play for big stakes!"

"Yes, we do," says Lady Perkins; "and when a person is playing for sums like that it ain't no time to trifle, especially when you're playing against an expert like Mrs. Snell."

"The game must be awfully exciting," said Ella. "I wished we could watch it sometime."

"I guess it wouldn't hurt nothing," says Perkie; "not if you kept still. Maybe you'd bring me luck."

"Was you going to play to-night?" asked Kate.

"No," says the Lady. "They's going to be a little dance here to-night and Mr. Snell's dance mad, so he insists on borrowing his wife for the occasion. Doctor Platt likes to dance too."

"We're all wild about it," says Kate. "Is this an invitation affair?"

"Oh, no," says Perk. "It's for the guests of the hotel."

Then she said good-by to us and went in the dining room. The rest of our conversation all day was about the dance and what should we wear, and how nice and democratic Lady Perkins was, and to hear her talk you wouldn't never know she had a title. I s'pose the gals thought she ought to stop every three or four steps and declare herself.

I made the announcement about noon that I wasn't going to partake in the grand ball. My corn was the alibi. But they wasn't no way to escape from dressing up and escorting the two gals into the grand ballroom and then setting there with them.

The dance was a knock-out. Outside of Ella and Kate and the aviator and myself, they was three couples. The Snells was there and so was Doctor Platt. He had a gal with him that looked like she might be his mother with his kid sister's clothes on. Then they was a pair of young shimmy shakers that ought to of been give their bottle and tucked in the hay at six p.m. A corn wouldn't of bothered them the way they danced; their feet wasn't involved in the transaction.

I and the Mrs. and Kate was the only ones there in evening clothes. The others had attended these functions before and knew that they wouldn't be enough suckers on hand to make any difference whether you wore a monkey suit or rompers. Besides, it wasn't Saturday night.

The music was furnished by the three-piece orchestra that usually done their murder in the summer parlor.

Ella was expecting me to introduce her and Kate to the Snell gal, but her and her husband was so keen for dancing that they called it off in the middle of the second innings and beat it upstairs. Then Ella said she wouldn't mind meeting Platt, but when he come past us and I spoke to him he give me a look like you would expect from a flounder that's been wronged.

So poor Codd danced one with Kate and one with Ella, and so on, and so on, till finally it got pretty late, a quarter to ten, and our party was the only merrymakers left in the joint. The orchestra looked over at us to see if we could stand some more punishment. The Mrs. told me to go and ask them to play a couple more dances before they quit. They done what I asked them, but maybe I got my orders mixed up.

The next morning I asked Wurz, the manager, how often the hotel give them dances.

"Oh," he says, "once or twice a month."

I told him I didn't see how they could afford it.

Kate went out after supper this next evening to take an automobile ride with Codd. So when I and Ella had set in the summer parlor a little wile, she proposed that we should go in and watch the bridge game. Well, I wasn't keen for it, but when you tell wife you don't want to do something she always says, "Why not?" and even if you've got a reason she'll make a monkey out of it. So we rapped at the door of the red card room and Lady Perkins said, "Come in," and in we went.

The two dudes and Mrs. Snell was playing with her again, but Perk was the only one that spoke.

"Set down," she said, "and let's see if you can bring me some luck."

So we drawed up a couple of chairs and set a little ways behind her. Her and the anonymous dude was partners against Doc and Mrs. Snell, and they didn't change all evening. I haven't played only a few games of bridge, but I know a little about it, and I never see such hands as Perkie held. It was a misdeal when she didn't have the ace, king and four or five others of one suit and a few picture cards and aces on the side. When she couldn't get the bid herself she doubled the other pair and made a sucker out of them. I don't know what they was playing a point, but when they broke up Lady Perkins and her dude was something like seven hundred berries to the good.

I and Ella went to bed wile they was settling up, but we seen her on the porch in the morning. She smiled at us and says: "You two are certainly grand mascots! I hope you can come in and set behind me again to-night. I ain't even yet, but one more run of luck like last night's and I'll be a winner. Then," she says, "I s'pose I'll have to give my mascots some kind of a treat."

Ella was tickled to death and couldn't hardly wait to slip Sis the good news. Kate had been out late and overslept herself and we was half through breakfast when she showed up. The Mrs. told her about the big game and how it looked like we was in strong with the nobility, and Kate said she had some good news of her own; that Codd had as good as told her he was stuck on her.

"And he's going to sell his invention for a million," says Ella. "So I guess we wasn't as crazy coming out to this place as some people thought we was."

"Wait till the machine's made good," I said.

"It has already," says Kate. "He was up in it yesterday and everything worked perfect and he says the Williamses was wild over it. And what do you think's going to come off to-morrow morning? He's going to take me up with him."

"Oh, no, Sis!" said Ella. "S'pose something should happen!"

"No hope," says I.

"But even if something should happen," said Katie, "what would I care as long as it happened to Bob and I together!"

I told the waitress to bring me another order of fried mush.

"To-night," said Kate, "Bob's going in Town to a theater party with some boys he went to college with. So I can help you bring Lady Perkins good luck."

Something told me to crab this proposition and I tried, but it was passed over my veto. So the best I could do was to remind Sis, just before we went in the gambling den, to keep her mouth shut wile the play was going on.

Perk give us a smile of welcome and her partner smiled too.

For an hour the game went along about even. Kate acted like she was bored, and she didn't have nothing to say after she'd told them, wile somebody was dealing, that she was going to have an aeroplane ride in the morning. Finally our side begin to lose, and lose by big scores. They was one time when they was about sixteen hundred points to the bad. Lady Perkins didn't seem to be enjoying herself and when Ella addressed a couple of remarks to her the cat had her tongue.

But the luck switched round again and Lady Perk had all but caught up when the blow-off come.

It was the rubber game, with the score nothing and nothing. The Doc dealt the cards. I was setting where I could see his hand and Perk's both. Platt had the king, jack and ten and five other hearts. Lady Perkins held the ace and queen of hearts, the other three aces and everything else in the deck.

The Doc bid two hearts. The other dude and Mrs. Snell passed.

"Two without," says Lady Perkins.

"Three hearts," says Platt.

The other two passed again and Perk says: "Three without."

Katie had came strolling up and was pretty near behind Perk's chair.

"Well," says Platt, "it looks like——"

But we didn't find out what it looked like, as just then Katie says: "Heavens! Four aces! Don't you wished you was playing penny ante?"

It didn't take Lady Perkins no time at all to forget her title.

"You fool!" she screams, w'eeling round on Kate. "Get out of here, and get out of here quick, and don't never come near me again! I hope your aeroplane falls a million feet. You little fool!"

I don't know how the hand come out. We wasn't there to see it played.

Lady Perkins got part of her hope. The aeroplane fell all right, but only a couple of miles instead of a million feet. They say that they was a defect or something in poor Codd's engine. Anyway, he done an involuntary nose dive. Him and his invention was spilled all over Long Island. But Katie had been awake all night with the hysterics and Ella hadn't managed to get her to sleep till nine a.m. So when Codd had called for her Ella'd told him that Sis would go some other day. Can you beat it?

Wile I and Ella was getting ready for supper I made the remark that I s'posed we'd live in a vale of tears for the next few days.

"No," said Ella. "Sis is taking it pretty calm. She's sensible. She says if that could of happened, why the invention couldn't of been no good after all. And the Williamses probably wouldn't of give him a plugged dime for it."

Lady Perkins didn't only speak to me once afterwards. I seen her setting on the porch one day, reading a book. I went up to her and said: "Hello." They wasn't no answer, so I thought I'd appeal to her sympathies.

"Maybe you're still interested in my dogs," I said. "They was too far gone and the veter'nary had to order them shot."

"That's good," said Perk, and went on reading.

IV

ONLY ONE

About a week after this, the Mrs. made the remark that the Decker wasn't big enough to hold both she and Perkins.

"She treats us like garbage," says the Mrs., "and if I stay here much longer I'll forget myself and do her nose in a braid."

But Perk left first and saved us the trouble. Her husband was down in Texas looking after some oil gag and he wired her a telegram one day to come and join him as it looked like he would have to stay there all summer. If I'd of been him I'd of figured that Texas was a sweet enough summer resort without adding your wife to it.

We was out on the porch when her ladyship and two dogs shoved off.

"Three of a kind," said the Mrs.

And she stuck her tongue out at Perk and felt like that made it all even. A woman won't stop at nothing to revenge insults. I've saw them stagger home in a new pair of 3 double A shoes because some fresh clerk told them the 7 Ds they tried on was too small. So anyway we decided to stay on at the Decker and the two gals prettied themselves up every night for dinner in the hopes that somebody besides the head-waiter would look at them twice, but we attracted about as much attention as a dirty finger nail in the third grade.

That is, up till Herbert Daley come on the scene.

Him and Katie spotted each other at the same time. It was the night he come to the Decker. We was pretty near through dinner when the head-waiter showed him to a table a little ways from us. The majority of the guests out there belongs to the silly sex and a new man is always a riot, even with the married ones. But Daley would of knocked them dead anywheres. He looked like he was born and raised in Shubert's chorus and the minute he danced in all the women folks forgot the feed bag and feasted their eyes on him. As for Daley, after he'd glanced at the bill of fare, he let his peepers roll over towards our table and then they quit rolling. A cold stare from Kate might have scared him off, but if they was ever a gal with "Welcome" embroidered on her pan, she's it.

It was all I could do to tear Ella and Sis from the dining room, though they was usually in a hurry to romp out to the summer parlor and enjoy a few snubs. I'd just as soon of set one place as another, only for the waitress, who couldn't quit till we did and she generally always had a date with the big ski jumper the hotel hires to destroy trunks.

Well, we went out and listened a wile to the orchestra, which had brought a lot of new jazz from the Prince of Pilsen, and we waited for the new dude to show up, but he didn't, and finally I went in to the desk to buy a couple of cigars and there he was, talking to Wurz, the manager. Wurz introduced us and after we'd shook hands Daley excused himself and said he was going upstairs to write a letter. Then Wurz told me he was Daley the horseman.

"He's just came up from the South," says Wurz. "He's going to be with us till the meetings is over at Jamaica and Belmont. He's got a whale of a stable and he expects to clean up round New York with Only One, which he claims can beat any horse in the world outside of Man o' War. They's some other good ones in the bunch, too, and he says he'll tell me when he's going to bet on them. I don't only bet once in a long wile and then never more than $25 at a crack, but I'll take this baby's tips as often as he comes through with them. I guess a man won't make no mistake following a bird that bets five and ten thousand at a clip, though of course it don't mean much to him if he win or lose. He's dirty with it."

I asked Wurz if Daley was married and he said no.

"And listen," he says: "It looks like your little sister-in-law had hit him for a couple of bases. He described where she was setting in the dining room and asked who she was."

"Yes," I said, "I noticed he was admiring somebody at our table, but I thought maybe it was me."

"He didn't mention you," says Wurz, "only to make sure you wasn't Miss Kate's husband."

"If he was smart he'd know that without asking," I said. "If she was my wife I'd be wearing weeds."

I went back to the gals and told them I'd met the guy. They was all steamed up.

"Who is he?" says Kate.

"His name is Herbert Daley," I told her. "He's got a stable over to Jamaica."

"A stable!" says Ella, dropping her jaw. "A man couldn't dress like he and run a livery."

So I had to explain that he didn't run no livery, but owned a string of race horses.

"How thrilling!" says Katie. "I love races! I went to the Grand Circuit once, the time I was in Columbus."

"These is different," I says. "These is thurlbreds."

"So was they thurlbreds!" she says. "You always think a thing can't be no good if you wasn't there."

I let her win that one.

"We must find out when the race is and go," said the Mrs.

"They's six of them every day," I said, "but it costs about five smackers apiece to get in, to say nothing about what you lose betting."

"Betting!" says Katie. "I just love to bet and I never lose. Don't you remember the bet I made with Sammy Pass on the baseball that time? I took him for a five-pound box of candy. I just felt that Cincinnati was going to win."

"So did the White Sox," I says. "But if you bet with the boys over to Jamaica, the only candy they'll take you for is an all-day sucker."

"What did Mr. Daley have to say?" asked Ella.

"He had to say he was pleased to meet me," I told her. "He proved it by chasing upstairs to write a letter."

"Probably to his wife," said Kate.

"No," I said. "Wurz tells me he ain't got no wife. But he's got plenty of jack, so Wurz says."

"Well, Sis," says the Mrs., "that's no objection to him, is it?"

"Don't be silly!" said Katie. "He wouldn't look at me."

"I guess not!" I says. "He was so busy doing it in the dining room, that half his soup never got past his chin. And listen: I don't like to get you excited, but Wurz told me he asked who you was."

"O Sis!" said the Mrs. "It looks like a Romance."

"Wurz didn't say nothing about a Romance," said I. "He may be interested like the rubes who stare with their mouth open at Ringling's 'Strange People.'"

"Oh, you can't tease Sis like that," said Ella. "She's as pretty as a picture to-night and nobody could blame a man from admiring her."

"Especially when we don't know nothing about him," I says. "He may be a snow-eater or his upstairs rooms is unfurnished or something."

"Well," says Ella, "if he shows up again to-night, don't you forget to introduce us."

"Better not be in no hurry," I said.

"Why not?" said Ella. "If him and Sis likes each other's looks, why, the sooner they get acquainted, it won't hurt nothing."

"I don't know," I says. "I've noticed that most of the birds you chose for a brother-in-law only stayed in the family as long as they was strangers."

"Nobody said nothing about Mr. Daley as a brother-in-law," says Ella.

"Oh!" I said. "Then I suppose you want Katie to meet him so as she can land a hostler's job."

Well, in about a half hour, the gals got their wish and Daley showed up. I didn't have to pull no strategy to land him. He headed right to where we was setting like him and I was old pals. I made the introductions and he drawed up a chair and parked. The rest of the guests stared at us goggle-eyed.

"Some hotel!" says Daley.

"We like it," says the Mrs. "They's so many nice people lives here."

"We know by hearsay," I said, but she stepped on my foot.

"It's handy for me," said Daley. "I have a few horses over to the Jamaica race track and it's a whole lot easier to come here than go in Town every night."

"Do you attend the races every day?" says Katie.

"Sure," he says. "It's my business. And they's very few afternoons when one of my nags ain't entered."

"My! You must have a lot of them!" said Kate.

"Not many," says Daley. "About a hundred. And I only shipped thirty."

"Imagine!" said Kate.

"The army's got that many," I said.

"The army ain't got none like mine," says Daley. "I guess they wished they had of had. I'd of been glad to of helped them out, too, if they'd asked me."

"That's why I didn't enlist," I said. "Pershing never even suggested it."

"Oh, I done my bit all right," says Daley. "Two hundred thousand in Liberty Bonds is all."

"Just like throwing it away!" I says.

"Two hundred thousand!" says Ella. "And you've still got money left?"

She said this in a joking way, but she kept the receiver to her ear.

"I ain't broke yet," says Daley, "and I don't expect to be."

"You don't half know this hotel," I says.

"The Decker does charge good prices," said Daley, "but still and all, a person is willing to pay big for the opportunity of meeting young ladies like the present company."

"O Mr. Daley!" said Kate. "I'm afraid you're a flatter."

"I bet he makes them pretty speeches to every woman he meets," says Ella.

"I haven't met none before who I felt like making them," says Daley.

Wile they was still talking along these lines, the orchestra begin to drool a Perfect Day, so I ducked out on the porch for air. The gals worked fast wile I was gone and when I come back it was arranged that Daley was to take us to the track next afternoon in his small car.

His small car was a toy that only had enough room for the people that finds fault with Wilson. I suppose he had to leave his big car in New York on account of the Fifty-ninth Street bridge being so frail.

Before we started I asked our host if they was a chance to get anything to drink over to the track and he says no, but pretty near everybody brought something along on the hip, so I said for them to wait a minute wile I went up to the room and filled a flask. When we was all in the car, the Mrs. wanted to know if it wasn't risky, me taking the hooch along.

"It's against the prohibition law," she says.

"So am I," I said.

"They's no danger," says Daley. "They ain't began to force prohibition yet. I only wished they had. It would save me a little worry about my boy."

"Your boy!" said Katie, dropping her jaw a foot.

"Well, I call him my boy," says Daley. "I mean little Sid Mercer, that rides for me. He's the duke of them all when he lays off the liquor. He's gave me his word that he won't touch nothing as long as he's under contract to me, and he's kept straight so far, but I can't help from worr'ing about him. He ought to be good, though, when I pay him $20,000 for first call, and leave him make all he can on the side. But he ain't got much stren'th of character, you might say, and if something upsets him, he's liable to bust things wide open.

"I remember once he was stuck on a gal down in Louisville and he was supposed to ride Great Scott for Bradley in the Derby. He was the only one that could handle Scott right, and with him up Scott would of win as far as from here to Dallas. But him and the gal had a brawl the day before the race and that night the kid got stiff. When it come time for the race he couldn't of kept a seat on a saw horse. Bradley had to hustle round and dig up another boy and Carney was the only one left that could ride at all and him and Great Scott was strangers. So Bradley lose the race and canned Mercer."

"Whisky's a terrible thing," says Ella. A woman'll sometimes pretend for a long wile like she's stupid and all of a sudden pull a wise crack that proves she's a thinker.

"Well," says Daley, "when Bradley give him the air, I took him, and he's been all right. I guess maybe I know how to handle men."

"Men only?" says Katie, smiling.

"Men and horses," said Daley. "I ain't never tried to handle the fair sex and I don't know if I could or not. But I've just met one that I think could handle me." And he give her a look that you could pour on a waffle.

Daley had a table saved for him in the clubhouse and we eat our lunch. The gals had clubhouse sandwiches, probably figuring they was caught fresh there. They was just one of Daley's horses entered that day and he told us he wasn't going to bet on it, as it hadn't never showed nothing and this was just a try-out. He said, though, that they was other horses on the card that looked good and maybe he would play them after he'd been round and talked to the boys.

"Yes," says Kate, "but the men you'll talk to knows all about the different horses and they'll tell you what horses to bet on and how can I win?"

"Why," says Daley, "if I decide to make a little bet on So-and-So I'll tell you about it and you can bet on the same horse."

"But if I'm betting with you," says Kate, "how can we bet on the same horse?"

"You're betting with me, but you ain't betting against me," said Daley. "This ain't a bet like you was betting with your sister on a football game or something. We place our bets with the bookmakers, that makes their living taking bets. Whatever horse we want to bet on, they take the bet."

"They must be crazy!" says Katie. "Your friends tell you what horse is going to win and you bet on them and the bookbinders is stung."

"My friends makes mistakes," says Daley, "and besides, I ain't the only guy out here that bets. Pretty near everybody at the track bets and the most of them don't know a race horse from a corn plaster. A bookmaker that don't finish ahead on the season's a cuckoo. Now," he says, "if you'll excuse me for a few minutes, I'll go down to the paddock and see what's new."

So wile he was gone we had a chance to look round and they was plenty to see. It was a Saturday and a big crowd out. Lots of them was gals that you'd have to have a pick to break through to their regular face. Since they had their last divorce, about the only excitement they could enjoy was playing a long shot. Which reminds me that they's an old saying that nobody loves a fat man, but you go out to a race track or down to Atlantic City or any place where the former wifes hangs out and if you'll notice the birds with them, the gents that broke up their home, you'll find out that the most of them is guys with chins that runs into five and six figures and once round their waist is a sleeper jump.

Besides the Janes and the fat rascals with them, you seen a flock of ham actors that looked like they'd spent the night in a Chinese snowstorm, and maybe a half a dozen losers'-end boxers that'd used the bridge of their nose to block with and always got up in the morning just after the clock had struck ten, thinking they'd been counted out.

Pretty near everybody wore a pair of field glasses on a strap and when the race was going on they'd look through them and tell the world that the horse they'd bet on was three len'ths in front and just as good as in, but I never heard of a bookie paying off on that dope, and personally when some one would insist on lending me a pair to look through I couldn't tell if the things out there racing was horses or gnats.

Daley was back with us in a few minutes and says to Kate: "I guess you'll have to bet on yourself in the first race."

So she asked him what did he mean and he said: "I had a tip on a filly named Sweet and Pretty."

"O Mr. Daley!" says Kate.

"They don't expect her to win," says Daley, "but she's six, two and even, and I'm going to play her place and show."

Then he explained what that was and he said he was going to bet a thousand each way and finally the gals decided to go in for $10 apiece to show. It tickled them to death to find out that they didn't have to put up nothing. We found seats down in front wile Daley went to place the bets. Pretty soon the horses come out and Kate and Ella both screamed when they seen how cute the jockeys was dressed. Sweet and Pretty was No. 10 and had a combination of colors that would knock your eye out. Daley come back and explained that every owner had their own colors and of course the gals wanted to know what his was and he told them Navy blue and orange sleeves with black whoops on them and a blue cap.

"How beautiful!" says Ella. "I can't hardly wait to see them!"

"You must have wonderful taste in colors!" says Kate.

"Not only in colors," he says.

"O Mr. Daley!" she says again.

Well, the race was ran and No. 10 was a Sweet and Pretty last.

"Now," I says, "you O Mr. Daley."

The gals had yelped themself hoarse and didn't have nothing to say, but I could tell from their face that it would take something more than a few pretty speeches to make up for that twenty men.

"Never mind that!" said Daley. "She got a rotten ride. We'll get that back on the next one."

His hunch in the next one was Sena Day and he was betting a thousand on her to place at 4 to 1. He made the gals go in for $20 apiece, though they didn't do it with no pep. I went along with him to place the bets and he introduced me to a bookie so as I could bet a few smackers of my own when I felt like it. You know they's a law against betting unless it's a little bet between friends and in order to be a bookie's friend he's got to know your name. A quick friendship sprung up between I and a guy named Joe Meyer, and he not only give me his card but a whole deck of them. You see the law also says that when you make one of these bets with your pals he can't give you no writing to show for it, but he's generally always a man that makes a lot of friends and it seems like they all want to make friendly bets with him, and he can't remember where all his buddies lives, so he makes them write their name and address on the cards and how much the friendly wager is for and who on, and so forth, and the next day he mails them the bad news and they mail him back a check for same. Once in a wile, of course, you get the bad news and forget to mail him the check and he feels blue over it as they's nothing as sad as breaking up an old friendship.

I laid off Sena Day and she win. Daley smiled at the gals.

"There!" he says. "I'm sorry we didn't play her on the nose, but I was advised to play safe."

"Fine advice!" said Kate. "It's cost Sis and I $60 so far."

"What do you mean?" says Daley.

"We lose $20 on the first race," she says, "and you tell us we'll get it back on the next one and we bet the horse'll come second and it don't."

So we had to explain that if a horse win, why it placed, too, and her and Ella had grabbed $160 on that race and was $140 ahead. He was $2,000 winners himself.

"We'll have a drink on Sena," he says. "I don't believe they was six people out here that bet a nickel on her."

So Katie told him he was wonderful and him and the gals had a sarsaparilla or something and I poured my own. He'd been touting Cleopatra in the third race, but her and everybody else was scratched out of it except Captain Alcock and On Watch. On Watch was 9 to 10 and Alcock even money and Daley wouldn't let us bet

"On Watch is best," he says, "but he's giving away twenty pounds and you can't tell. Anyway, it ain't worth it at that price."

"Only two horses in the race?" asked Ella.

"That's all," he says.

"Well, then, listen," she says, all excited: "Why not bet on one of them for place?"

Daley laughed and said it was a grand idear only he didn't think the bookbinders would stand for it.

"But maybe they don't know," she says.

"I guess they do," said Daley. "It's almost impossible to keep a secret like that round a race track."

"Besides," I said, "the bookworms owes you and Kate $70 apiece and if you put something like that over on them and they find it out, they'll probably get even by making you a check on the West Bank of the Hudson River."

So we decided to play fair and lay off the race entirely. On Watch come through and the gals felt pretty bad about it till we showed them that they'd of only grabbed off nine smackers apiece if they'd of plunged on him for $20 straight.

Along toward time for the next race, Daley steered us down by the paddock and we seen some of the nags close up. Daley and the gals raved over this one and that one, and wasn't this one a beauty, and so forth. Personally they was all just a horse to me and I never seen one yet that wasn't homelier than the City Hall. If they left it up to me to name the world's champion eyesore, I'd award the elegant barb' wire wash rag to a horse rode by a woman in a derby hat. People goes to the Horse Show to see the Count de Fault; they don't know a case of withers from an off hind hock. And if the Sport of Kings was patronized by just birds that admires equine charms, you could park the Derby Day crowd in a phone booth.

A filly named Tamarisk was the favorite in the fourth race and Daley played her for eight hundred smackers at 4 to 5. The gals trailed along with $8 apiece and she win from here to Worcester. The fifth was the one that Daley had an entry in—a dog named Fly-by-Night. It was different in the daytime. Mercer had the mount and done the best he could, which was finish before supper. Nobody bet, so nobody was hurt.

"He's just a green colt," Daley told us. "I wanted to see how he'd behave."

"Well," I said, "I thought he behaved like a born caboose."

Daley liked the Waterbury entry in the last and him and the gals played it and win. All told, Daley was $4,000 ahead on the day and Ella and Kate had picked up $160 between them. They wanted to kiss everybody on the way out. Daley sent us to the car to wait for him. He wanted to see Mercer a minute. After a wile he come out and brought Mercer along and introduced him. He's a good-looking kid only for a couple of blotches on his pan and got an under lip and chin that kind of lags behind. He was about Kate's height, and take away his Adams apple and you could mail him to Duluth for six cents. Him and Kate got personal right away and she told him how different he looked now than in his riding make-up. He said he had a new outfit that he'd of wore if he'd knew she was looking on. So I said I hoped he didn't expect to ride Fly-by-Night round the track and keep a suit new, and he laughed, and Daley didn't seem to enjoy the conversation and said we'd have to be going, but when we started off, Kate and Mercer give each other a smile with a future in it. She's one of these gals that can't help from looking open house, even if the guy takes after a pelican.

Daley moved to our table that night and after that we eat breakfast and supper with him pretty near every day. After breakfast the gals would go down to New York to spend what they had win the day before, and I'll admit that Daley give us many a winner. I begin betting a little of my own jack, but I stuck the proceeds in the old sock. I ain't superstitious about living off a woman's money as long as you're legally married, but at the clip the two gals was going, it looked like their old man's war profits was on the way to join their maker, and the more jack I laid by, the less sooner I would have to go to work.

We'd meet every afternoon at the track and after the races Daley'd bring us back to the hotel. After supper we'd set round and chin or play rummy or once in a wile we'd go in Town to a show or visit one of the road houses near the Decker. The mail service on Long Island's kind of rotten and they's a bunch of road houses that hasn't heard of prohibition.

During the time we'd lived in Town Katie had got acquainted with three or four birds that liked her well enough to take her places where they wasn't no cover charge, but since we'd moved to the Decker we hadn't heard from none of them. That is, till a few days after we'd met Daley, when she told us that one of the New York boys, a guy named Goldberg, had called up and wanted her to come in and see a show with him. He's a golf champion or something. Well, Daley offered to drive her in, but she said no, she'd rather go on the train and Goldberg was going to meet her. So she went, and Daley tried to play cards with Ella and I, but he was too restless and finally snuck up to his room.

They wasn't no question about his feelings toward Kate. He was always trying to fix it to be alone with her, but I guess it was the first time in her life when she didn't have to do most of the leading and she kept him at arm's len'th. Her and Ella had many a battle. Ella told her that the first thing she knowed he'd get discouraged and walk out on her; that she'd ought to quit monking and give him to understand that she was ready to yes him when he spoke up. But Katie said she guessed she could run her own love affairs as she'd had a few more of them than Ella.

So Ella says: "Maybe you have, but which one of us has got the husband?"

"You, thank the Lord!" says Katie.

"Thank him twice," I said.

Kate didn't come home from her New York party till two o'clock and she overslept herself till it was too late to go down again and shop. So we all drove over to the track with Daley and most of the way over he acted like a child. Katie kept talking about what a good show she seen and had a grand time, and so forth, and he pretended he wasn't listening. Finally she cut it out and give him the old oil and by the time we got to the clubhouse he'd tossed in the sponge.

That was the last day at Jamaica and a couple of his horses was in. We was all down on them and they both copped, though Mercer had to give one of them a dude ride to pull us through. Daley got maudlin about what a grand rider the kid was and a grand little fella besides, and he had half a notion to bring him along with us back to the hotel and show him a good time. But Kate said what was the use of an extra man, as it would kind of spoil things and she was satisfied with just Daley. So of course that tickled him and everybody was feeling good and after supper him and Kate snuck out alone for the first time. Ella made me set up till they come back, so as she could get the news. Well, Daley had asked her all right, but she told him she wanted a little wile to think.

"Think!" says Ella. "What does she want to think for?"

"The novelty, I suppose," said I.

Only One was in the big stake race the next day, when we shifted over to Belmont. They was five or six others in with him, all of them pretty good, and the price on him was 3 to 1.

He hadn't started yet since Daley'd brought him here, but they'd been nursing him along and Mercer and the trainer said he was right.

I suppose of course you've been out to Belmont. At that time they run the wrong way of the track, like you deal cards. Daley's table was in a corner of the clubhouse porch and when you looked up the track, the horses was coming right at you. Even the boys with the trick glasses didn't dast pretend they could tell who's ahead.

The Belmont national hymn is Whispering. The joint's so big and scattered round that a German could sing without disturbing the party at the next table. But they seems to be a rule that when they's anything to be said, you got to murmur it with the lips stuck to the opponent's earlobe. They shush you if you ask out loud for a toothpick. Everywheres you'll see two or three guys with their heads together in a whispering scene. One of them has generally always just been down to the horses' dining room and had lunch with Man o' War or somebody and they told him to play Sea Mint in the next race as Cleopatra had walked the stall all night with her foal. A little ways off they'll be another pair of shushers and one of them's had a phone call from Cleopatra's old dam to put a bet on Cleo as Captain Alcock had got a hold of some wild oats and they couldn't make him do nothing but shimmy.

If they's ten horses in a race you can walk from one end of the clubhouse to the other and get a whisper on all ten of them. I remember the second time Man o' War run there. They was only one horse that wanted to watch him from the track and the War horse was 1 to 100. So just before the race, if you want to call it that, I seen a wise cracker that I'd got acquainted with, that had always been out last night with Madden or Waterbury, so just kidding I walked up to him and asked him who he liked. So he motioned me to come over against the wall where they wasn't nobody near us and whispered, "Man o' War's unbeatable." You see if that remark had of been overheard and the news allowed to spread round, it might of forced the price to, say, 1 to a lump of coal, and spoiled the killing.

Well, wile the Jamaica meeting was on, the gals had spent some of their spare time figuring out how much they'd of been ahead if Daley had of let them bet more than ten to twenty smackers a race. So this day at Belmont, they said that if he liked Only One so much, he should ought to leave them raise the ante just once and play fifty apiece.

But he says: "No, not this time. I'm pretty sure he'll win, but he's in against a sweet field and he ain't raced for a month. I'll bet forty on the nose for the two of you, and if he looks good you can gamble some real money the next time he runs."

So Ella and Kate had to be satisfied with $20 apiece. Daley himself bet $2,000 and I piked along with $200 that I didn't tell the gals nothing about. We all got 3 to 1. A horse named Streak of Lightning was favorite at 6 to 5. It was a battle. Only One caught the Streak in the last step and win by a flea's jaw. Everybody was in hysterics and the gals got all messed up clawing each other.

"Nobody but Mercer could of did it!" says Daley, as soon as he could talk.

"He's some jockey!" yelled Kate. "O you Sid!"

Pretty soon the time was give out and Only One had broke the track record for the distance, whatever it was.

"He's a race horse!" said Daley. "But it's too bad he had to extend himself. We won't get no price the next time out."

Well, altogether the race meant $14,000 to Daley, and he said we'd all go to Town that night and celebrate. But when we got back to the Decker, they was a telegram for him and he had to pack up and beat it for Kentucky.

Daley being away didn't stop us from going to the track. He'd left orders with Ernest, his driver, to take us wherever we wanted to go and the gals had it so bad now that they couldn't hardly wait till afternoon. They kept on trimming the books, too. Kate got a phone call every morning that she said was from this Goldberg and he was giving her tips. Her and Ella played them and I wished I had. I would of if I'd knew who they was from. They was from Mercer, Daley's boy. That's who they was from.

I and Ella didn't wise up till about the third night after Daley'd went. That night, Kate took the train to Town right after supper, saying she had a date with Goldberg. It was a swell night and along about eight, I and Ella decided we might as well have a ride. So we got a hold of Ernest and it wound up by us going to New York too. We seen a picture and batted round till midnight and then Ella says why not go down to the Pennsylvania Station and pick Kate up when she come to take the train, and bring her home. So we done it. But when Katie showed up for the train, it was Mercer that was with her, not Goldberg.

Well, Mercer was pretty near out to the car with us when he happened to think that Daley's driver mustn't see him. So he said good night and left us. But he didn't do it quick enough. Daley's driver had saw him and I seen that he'd saw him and I knowed that he wasn't liable to be stuck on another of Daley's employs that was getting ten times as much money as him and all the cheers, and never had to dirty himself up changing a tire. And I bet it was all Ernest could do was wait till Daley come back so as he could explode the boom.

Kate and Ella didn't know Ernest was hep and I didn't tell them for fear of spoiling the show, so the women done their brawling on the way home in a regular race track whisper. The Mrs. told Kate she was a hick to be monking round with a jockey when Daley was ready and willing to give her a modern home with a platinum stopper in the washbowl. Kate told Ella that she wasn't going to marry nobody for their money, and besides, Mercer was making more than enough to support a wife, and how that boy can dance!

"But listen," she says: "I ain't married to neither one of them yet and don't know if I want to be."

"Well," says Ella, "you won't have no chance to marry Daley if he finds out about you and Mercer."

"He won't find out unless you tell him," said Kate.

"Well, I'll tell him," says Ella, "unless you cut this monkey business out."

"I'll cut it out when I get good and ready," says Kate. "You can tell Daley anything you please."

She knew they wasn't no chance of Ella making good.

"Daley'll be back in a couple of days," says the Mrs. "When he comes he'll want his answer and what are you going to say?"

"Yes or no, according to which way I make up my mind," said Kate. "I don't know yet which one I like best."

"That's ridic'lous!" Ella says. "When a girl says she can't make up her mind, it shows they's nothing to make up. Did you ever see me when I couldn't make up my mind?"

"No," said Katie, "but you never had even one whole man to choose between."

The last half of the ride neither of them were talking. That's a world's record in itself. They kind of made up the next morning after I'd told Ella that the surest way to knock Daley's chances for a gool was to paste Mercer.

"Just lay off of it," I told her. "The best man'll win in fair competition, which it won't be if you keep plugging for Daley."

We had two more pretty fair days at the track on Kate's tips that Mercer give her. We also went on a party with him down Town, but we used the train, not Daley's car.

Daley showed up on a Wednesday morning and had Ernest take him right over to the track. I suppose it was on this trip that Ernest squealed. Daley didn't act no different when we joined him on the clubhouse porch, but that night him and Kate took a ride alone and come back engaged.

They'd been pointing Only One for the Merrick Handicap, the fourth race on Saturday. It was worth about $7,000 to the winner. The distance was seven furlongs and Only One had top weight, 126 pounds. But Thursday he done a trial over the distance in 1.22, carrying 130 pounds, so it looked like a set-up.

Thursday morning I and Ella happened to be in Katie's room when the telephone rung. It was Mercer on the other end. He asked her something and she says: "I told you why in my note."

So he said something else and she says: "Not with no jail-bird."

And she hung up.

Well, Ella wanted to know what all the pleasantries was about, but Kate told her to mind her own business.

"You got your wish and I'm engaged to Daley," she says, "and that's all you need to know."

For a gal that was going to marry a dude that was supposed to have all the money in the world, she didn't act just right, but she wouldn't been Kate if she had of, so I didn't think much about it.

Friday morning I got a wire from one of the South Bend boys, Goat Anderson, sent from Buffalo, saying he'd be in New York that night and would I meet him at the Belmont at seven o'clock. So I went in Town from the track and waited round till pretty near nine, but he didn't show up. I started to walk across to the Pennsylvania Station and on the way I dropped in at a place where they was still taking a chance. I had one up at the bar and was throwing it into me when a guy in the back part yelled "Hey! Come here!" It was Mercer yelling and it was me he wanted.

He was setting at a table all alone with a highball. It didn't take no Craig Kennedy to figure out that it wasn't his first one.

"Set down before I bat you down!" he says.

"Listen," I says: "I wished you was champion of the world. You'd hold onto the title just long enough for me to reach over and sock you where most guys has a chin."

"Set down!" he says. "It's your wife I'm going to beat up, not you."

"You ain't going to beat up nobody's wife or nobody's husband," I says, "and if you don't cut out that line of gab you'll soon be asking the nurse how you got there."

"Set down and come clean with me," he says. "Was your wife the one that told Daley about your sister-in-law and I?"

"If she did, what of it?" I says.

"I'm asking you, did she?" he says.

"No, she didn't," I said. "If somebody told him his driver told him. He seen you the other night."

"Ernest!" he says. "Frank and Ernest! I'll Ernest him right in the jaw!"

"You're a fine matchmaker!" I says. "He could knock you for a row of flat tires. Why don't you try and get mad at Dempsey?"

"Set down and have a drink," says Mercer.

"I didn't mean that about your wife. You and her has treated me all right. And your sister-in-law, too, even if she did give me the air. And called me a jailbird. But that's all right. It's Daley I'm after and it's Daley I'm going to get."

"Sweet chance! "I says. "What could you do to him?"

"Wait and see!" said Mercer, and smiled kind of silly.

"Listen," I says. "Have you forgot that you're supposed to ride Only One to-morrow?"

"Supposed to ride is right," he says, and smiled again.

"Ain't you going to ride him?" I said.

"You bet I am!" he says.

"Well, then," I said, "you better call it a day and go home."

"I'm over twenty-one," he says, "and I'm going to set here and enjoy myself. But remember, I ain't keeping you up."

Well, they wasn't nothing I could do only set there and wait for him to get stiff and then see him to his hotel. We had a drink and we had another and a couple more. Finally he opened up. I wished you could of heard him. It took him two hours to tell his story, and everything he said, he said it over and over and repeated it four and five times. And part of the time he talked so thick that I couldn't hardly get him.

"Listen," he says. "Can you keep a secret? Listen," he says. "I'm going to take a chance with you on account of your sister-in-law. I loved that little gal. She's give me the air, but that don't make no difference; I loved that little gal and I don't want her to lose no money. So I'm going to tell you a secret and if you don't keep your clam shut I'll roll you for a natural. In the first place," he says, "how do you and Daley stack up?"

"That ain't no secret," I said. "I think he's all right. He'd been a good friend of mine."

"Oh," says Mercer, "so he's been a good friend of yours, has he? All right, then. I'm going to tell you a secret. Do you remember the day I met you and the gals in the car? Well, a couple of days later, Daley was feeling pretty good about something and he asked me how I liked his gal? So I told him she looked good. So he says, 'I'm going to marry that gal,' he says. He says, 'She likes me and her sister and brother-in-law is encouraging it along,' he says. 'They know I've got a little money and they're making a play for me. They're a couple of rats and I'm the cheese. They're going to make a meal off of me. They think they are,' he says. 'But the brother-in-law's a smart Aleck that thinks he's a wise cracker. He'd be a clown in a circus, only that's work. And his wife's fishing for a sucker with her sister for bait. Well, the gal's a pip and I'm going to marry her,' he says, 'but as soon as we're married, it's good-by, family-in-law! Me and them is going to be perfect strangers. They think they'll have free board and lodging at my house,' he says, 'but they won't get no meal unless they come to the back door for it, and when they feel sleepy they can make up a lower for themself on my cement porch.' That's the kind of a friend of yours this baby is," says Mercer.

I didn't say nothing and he went on.

"He's your friend as long as he can use you," he says. "He's been my friend since I signed to ride for him, that is, up till he found out I was stealing his gal. Then he shot my chances for a bull's-eye by telling her about a little trouble I had, five or six years ago. I and a girl went to a party down in Louisville and I seen another guy wink at her and I asked him what he meant by it and he said he had St. Vitus' dance. So I pulled the iron and knocked off a couple of his toes, to cure him. I was in eleven months and that's what Daley told Kate about. And of course he made her promise to not tell, but she wrote me a good-by note and spilled it. That's the kind of a pal he is.

"After I got out I worked for Bradley, and when Bradley turned me loose, he give me a $10,000 contract."

"He told us twenty," I said.

"Sure he did," says Mercer, "He always talks double. When he gets up after a tough night, both his heads aches. And if he ever has a baby he'll invite you over to see the twins. But anyway, what he pays me ain't enough and after to-morrow I'm through riding. What's ten or fifteen thousand a year when you can't drink nothing and you starve to death for the fear you'll pick up an ounce! Listen," he says. "I got a brother down in Oklahoma that's in the oil lease game. He cleaned up $25,000 last year and he wants me to go in with him. And with what I've saved up and what I'm going to win tomorrow, I should worry if we don't make nothing in the next two years."

"How are you going to win to-morrow?" I said. "The price'll be a joke."

"The price on who?" says Mercer.

"Only One," I said.

He give a silly laugh and didn't say nothing for a minute. Then he asked if Daley done the betting for I and the two gals. I told him he had did it at first, but now I was doing it.

"Well," he says, "you do it to-morrow, see? That little lady called me a jailbird, but I don't want her to lose her money."

So I asked him what he meant and he asked me for the tenth or eleventh time if I could keep a secret. He made me hold up my hand and swear I wouldn't crack what he was going to tell me.

"Now," he says, "what's the name of the horse I'm riding to-morrow?"

"Only One," I said.

"That ain't all of it," said Mercer. "His name to-morrow is Only One Left. See? Only One Left."

"Do you mean he's going to get left at the post?" I says.

"You're a Ouija board!" says Mercer. "Your name is Ouija and the horse's name is Only One Left. And listen," he says. "Everything but three horses is going to be scratched out of this race and we'll open at about 1 to 3 and back up to 1 to 5. And Daley's going to bet his right eye. But they's a horse in the race named Sap and that's the horse my two thousand smackers is going down on. And you're a sap, too, if you don't string along with me."

"Suppose you can't hold Only One?"

"Get the name right," said Mercer. "Only One Left. And don't worry about me not handling him. He thinks I'm Billy Sunday and everything I say he believes. Do you remember the other day when I beat Streak of Lightning? Well, the way I done that was whispering in One's ear, coming down the stretch. I says to him, 'One,' I says, 'this Lightning hoss has been spilling it round that your father's grandmother was a zebra. Make a bum out of him!' That's what I whispered to him and he got sore and went past Lightning like he was standing still. And to-morrow, just before we're supposed to go, I'll say to him, 'One, we're back at Jamaica. You're facing the wrong way.' And when Sap and the other dog starts, we'll be headed towards Rhode Island and in no hurry to get there."

"Mercer," I said, "I don't suppose they's any use talking to you, but after all, you're under contract to give Daley the best you've got and it don't look to me just like you was treating him square."

"Listen!" he says. "Him and square don't rhyme. And besides, I won't be under contract to nobody by this time tomorrow. So you save your sermon for your own parish."

I don't know if you'll think I done right or not. Or I don't care. But what was the sense of me tipping off a guy that had said them sweet things about I and Ella? And even if I don't want a sister-in-law of mine running round with a guy that's got a jail record, still Daley squealing on him was rotten dope. And besides, I don't never like to break a promise, especially to a guy that shoots a man's toes off just for having St Vitus' dance.

Well, anyway, the third race was over and the Merrick Handicap was next, and just like Mercer had said, they all quit but our horse and Sap and a ten-ton truck named Honor Bright. He was 20 to 1 and Sap was 6. Only One was 1 to 3 and Daley hopped on him with fifteen thousand men. Before post time the price was 1 to 5 and 1 to 6.

Daley was off his nut all afternoon and didn't object when I said I'd place the gals' money and save him the trouble. Kate and Ella had figured out what they had win up to date. It was about $1,200 and Daley told them to bet it all.

"You'll only make $400 between you," he says, "but it's a cinch."

"And four hundred's pretty good interest on $1,200," says Kate. "About ten per cent, ain't it?"

I left them and went downstairs. I wrote out a card for a hundred smackers on Sap. Then my feet caught cold and I didn't turn it in. I walked down towards the paddock and got there just as the boys was getting ready to parade. I seen Mercer and you wouldn't of never knew he'd fell off the wagon.

Daley was down there, too, and I heard him say: "Well, Sid, how about you?"

"Never better," says Mercer. "If I don't win this one I'll quit riding."

Then he seen me and smiled.

I chased back to the clubhouse, making up my mind on the way. I decided to not bet a nickel for the gals on anything. If Mercer was crossing me, I'd give Ella and Kate their $400 like they had win it, and say nothing. Personally, I was going to turn in the card I'd wrote on Sap. That was my idear when I got to Joe Meyer. But all of a sudden I had the hunch that Mercer was going through; they wasn't a chance in the world for him to weaken. I left Meyer's stand and went to a bookie named Haynes, who I'd bet with before.

Sap had went up to 8 to 1, and instead of a hundred smackers I bet a thousand.

He finished ahead by three len'ths, probably the most surprised horse in history. Honor Bright got the place, but only by a hair. Only One, after being detained for some reason another, come faster at the end than any horse ever run before. And Mercer give him an unmerciful walloping, pretending to himself, probably, that the hoss was its master.

We come back to our table. The gals sunk down in their chairs. Ella was blubbering and Kate was as white as a ghost. Daley finally joined us, looking like he'd had a stroke. He asked for a drink and I give him my flask.

"I can't understand it!" he says. "I don't know what happened!"

"You don't!" hollered Kate. "I'll tell you what happened You stole our money! Twelve hundred dollars! You cheat!"

"Oh, shut your fool mouth!" says Daley.

And another Romance was knocked for a row of sour apple trees.

Kate brought the mail in the dining room Monday morning. They was a letter for her and one for me. She read hers and they was a couple of tears in her eyes.

"Mercer's quit riding," she says. "This is a farewell note. He's going to Oklahoma."

Ella picked up my envelope.

"Who's this from?" she says.

"Give it here," I said, and took it away from her. "It's just the statement from Haynes, the bookie."

"Well, open it up," she said.

"What for?" said I. "You know how much you lose, don't you?"

"He might of made a mistake, mightn't he?" she says.

So I opened up the envelope and there was the check for $8,000.

"Gosh!" I said. "It looks like it was me that made the mistake!" And I laid the check down where her and Kate could see it. They screamed and I caught Ella just as she was falling off the chair.

"What does this mean?" says Kate.

"Well," I said, "I guess I was kind of rattled Saturday, and when I come to make my bet I got balled up and wrote down Sap. And I must of went crazy and played him for a thousand men."

"But where's our statement, mine and Sis'?" says Ella.

"That's my mistake again," I said. "I wrote out your ticket, but I must of forgot to turn it in."

They jumped up and come at me, and before I could duck I was kissed from both sides at once.

"O Sis!" yelps the Mrs. "Just think! We didn't lose our twelve hundred! We didn't lose nothing at all. We win eight thousand dollars!"

"Try and get it!" I says.

V

KATIE WINS A HOME

Oh yes, we been back here quite a wile. And we're liable to be here quite a wile. This town's good enough for me and it suits the Mrs. too, though they didn't neither one of us appreciate it till we'd give New York a try. If I was running the South Bend Boosters' club, I'd make everybody spend a year on the Gay White Way. They'd be so tickled when they got to South Bend that you'd never hear them razz the old burg again. Just yesterday we had a letter from Katie, asking us would we come and pay her a visit. She's a regular New Yorker now. Well, I didn't have to put up no fight with my Mrs. Before I could open my pan she says, "I'll write and tell her we can't come; that you're looking for a job and don't want to go nowheres just now."

Well, they's some truth in that. I don't want to go nowheres and I'll take a job if it's the right kind. We could get along on the interest from Ella's money, but I'm tired of laying round. I didn't do a tap of work all the time I was east and I'm out of the habit, but the days certainly do drag when a man ain't got nothing to do and if I can find something where I don't have to travel, I'll try it out.

But the Mrs. has still got most of what the old man left her and all and all, I'm glad we made the trip. I more than broke even by winning pretty close to $10,000 on the ponies down there. And we got Katie off our hands, which was one of the objects of us going in the first place—that and because the two gals wanted to see Life. So I don't grudge the time we spent, and we had some funny experiences when you look back at them. Anybody does that goes on a tour like that with a cuckoo like Katie. You hear a lot of songs and gags about mother-in-laws. But I could write a book of them about sister-in-laws that's twenty years old and pretty and full of peace and good will towards Men.

Well, after the blow-off with Daley, Long Island got too slow, besides costing us more than we could afford. So the gals suggested moving back in Town, to a hotel called the Graham on Sixty-seventh Street that somebody had told them was reasonable.

They called it a family hotel, but as far as I could see, Ella and I was the only ones there that had ever forced two dollars on the clergy. Outside of the transients, they was two song writers and a couple of gals that had their hair pruned and wrote for the papers, and the rest of the lodgers was boys that had got penned into a sixteen-foot ring with Benny Leonard by mistake. They looked like they'd spent many an evening hanging onto the ropes during the rush hour.

When we'd staid there two days, Ella and Katie was ready to pack up again.

"This is just a joint," said Ella. "The gals may be all right, but they're never in, only to sleep. And the men's impossible; a bunch of low prize-fighters."

I was for sticking, on account of the place being cheap, so I said:

"Second prize ain't so low. And you're overlooking the two handsome tune thiefs. Besides, what's the difference who else lives here as long as the rooms is clean and they got a good restaurant? What did our dude cellmates out on Long Island get us? Just trouble!"

But I'd of lose the argument as usual only for Kate oversleeping herself. It was our third morning at the Graham and her and Ella had it planned to go and look for a better place. But Katie didn't get up till pretty near noon and Ella went without her. So it broke so's Sis had just came downstairs and turned in her key when the two bellhops reeled in the front door bulging with baggage and escorting Mr. Jimmy Ralston. Yes, Jimmy Ralston the comedian. Or comic, as he calls it.

"Well, he ain't F.X. Bushman, as you know. But no one that seen him could make the mistake of thinking he wasn't somebody. And he looked good enough to Kate so as she waited till the clerk had him fixed up, and then ast who he was. The clerk told her and she told us when the Mrs. come back from her hunt. Ella begin to name a few joints where we might move, but it seemed like Sis had changed her mind.

"Oh," she says, "let's stay here a wile longer, a week anyway."

"What's came over you!" ast Ella. "You just said last night that you was bored to death here."

"Maybe we won't be so bored now," said Kate, smiling. "The Graham's looking up. We're entertaining a celebrity— Jimmy Ralston of the Follies."

Well, they hadn't none of us ever seen him on the stage, but of course we'd heard of him. He'd only just started with the Follies, but he'd made a name for himself at the Winter Garden, where he broke in two or three years ago. And Kate said that a chorus gal she'd met—Jane Abbott—had told her about Ralston and what a scream he was on a party.

"He's terribly funny when he gets just the right number of drinks," says Kate.

"Well, let's stay then," says Ella. "It'll be exciting to know a real actor."

"I would like to know him," says Katie, "not just because he's on the stage, but I think it'd be fun to set and listen to him talk. He must say the screamingest things! If we had him round we wouldn't have to play cards or nothing for entertainment. Only they say it makes people fat to laugh."

"If I was you, I'd want to get fat," I said. "Looking like an E string hasn't started no landslide your way."

"Is he attractive?" ast the Mrs.

"Well," said Kate, "he isn't handsome, but he's striking looking. You wouldn't never think he was a comedian. But then, ain't it generally always true that the driest people have sad faces?"

"That's a joke!" I said. "Did you ever see Bryan when he didn't look like somebody was tickling his feet?"

"We'll have to think up some scheme to get introduced to him," says Ella.

"It'll be tough," I says. "I don't suppose they's anybody in the world harder to meet than a member of the Follies, unless it's an Elk in a Pullman washroom."

"But listen," says Kate: "We don't want to meet him till we've saw the show. It'd be awfully embarrassing to have him ask us how we liked the Follies and we'd have to say we hadn't been to it."

"Yes," said the Mrs., "but still if we tell him we haven't been to it, he may give us free passes."

"Easy!" I said. "And it'd take a big load off his mind. They say it worries the Follies people half sick wondering what to do with all their free passes."

"Suppose we go to-night!" says Kate. "We can drop in a hotel somewheres and get seats. The longer we don't go, the longer we won't meet him."

"And the longer we don't meet him," I says, "the longer till he gives you the air."

"I'm not thinking of Mr. Ralston as a possible suitor," says Katie, swelling up. "But I do want to get acquainted with a man that don't bore a person to death."

"Well," I says, "if this baby's anything like the rest of your gentleman friends, he won't hardly be round long enough for that."

I didn't make no kick about going to the show. We hadn't spent no money since we'd moved back to Town and I was as tired as the gals of setting up in the room, playing rummy. They said we'd have to dress, and I kicked just from habit, but I'd got past minding that end of it. They was one advantage in dolling up every time you went anywheres. It meant an hour when they was no chance to do something even sillier.

We couldn't stop to put on the nose bag at the Graham because the women was scared we'd be too late to get tickets. Besides, when you're dressed for dinner, you at least want the waiter to be the same. So we took a taxi down to the Spencer, bought Follies seats in the ninth row, and went in to eat. It's been in all the papers that the price of food has came down, but the hotel man can't read. They fined us eleven smackers for a two-course banquet that if the Woman's Guild, here, would dast soak you four bits a plate for it, somebody'd write a nasty letter to the News-Times.

We got in the theater a half hour before the show begin. I put in the time finding out what the men will wear, and the gals looked up what scenes Ralston'd be in. He was only on once in each act. They don't waste much time on a comedian in the Follies. It don't take long to spring the two gags they can think up for him in a year, and besides, he just interferes with the big gal numbers, where Bunny Granville or somebody dreams of the different flappers he danced with at the prom, and the souvenirs they give him; and one by one the different gals writhes in, dressed like the stage director thinks they dress at the female colleges—a Wesley gal in pink tights, a Vassar dame in hula-hula, and a Smith gal with a sombrero and a sailor suit. He does a couple of steps with them and they each hand him a flower or a vegetable to remember them by. The song winds up:

> *But my most exclusive token*
> *Is a little hangnail broken*
> *Off the gal from Gussie's School for Manicures.*

And his real sweet patootie comes on made up as a scissors.

You've saw Ralston? He's a good comedian; no getting away from that. The way he fixes up his face, you laugh just to look at him. I yelled when I first seen him. He was supposed to be an office boy and he got back late from lunch and the boss ast him what made him late and he said he stopped to buy the extra. So the boss ast him what extra and he says the extra about the New York society couple getting married. So the boss said, "Why, they wouldn't print an extra about that. They's a New York society couple married most every day." So Ralston said, "Yes, but this couple is both doing it for the first time."

I don't remember what other gags he had, and they're old anyway by now. But he was a hit, especially with Ella and Kate. They screamed so loud I thought we'd get the air. If he didn't say a word, he'd be funny with that fool make-up and that voice.

I guess if it wasn't for me the gals would of insisted on going back to the stage door after the show and waiting for him to come out. I've saw Katie bad a lot of times, but never as cuckoo as this. It wasn't no case of love at first or second sight. You couldn't be stuck on this guy from seeing him. But she'd always been kind of stage-struck and was crazy over the idear of getting acquainted with a celebrity, maybe going round to places with him, and having people see her with Jimmy Ralston, the comedian. And then, of course, most anybody wants to meet a person that can make you laugh.

I managed to persuade them that the best dope would be to go back to the Graham and wait for him to come home; maybe we could fix it up with the night clerk to introduce us. I told them that irregardless of what you read in books, they's some members of the theatrical profession that occasionally visits the place where they sleep. So we went to the hotel and set in the lobby for an hour and a half, me trying to keep awake wile the gals played Ralston's part of the show over again a couple thousand times. They's nothing goes so big with me as listening to people repeat gags out of a show that I just seen.

The clerk had been tipped off and when Ralston finally come in and went to get his key, I strolled up to the desk like I was after mine. The clerk introduced us.

"I want you to meet my wife and sister-in-law," I said.

"Some other time," says Ralston. "They's a matinée tomorrow and I got to run off to bed."

So off he went and I got bawled out for Ziegfeld having matinées. But I squared myself two days afterwards when we went in the restaurant for lunch. He was just having breakfast and the three of us stopped by his table. I don't think he remembered ever seeing me before, but anyway he got up and shook hands with the women. Well, you couldn't never accuse Ella of having a faint heart, and she says:

"Can't we set down with you, Mr. Ralston? We want to tell you how much we enjoyed the Follies."

So he says, sure, set down, but I guess we would of anyway.

"We thought it was a dandy show," says Katie.

"It ain't a bad troupe," says Ralston.

"If you'll pardon me getting personal," said Ella, "we thought you was the best thing in it."

He looked like he'd strain a point and forgive her.

"We all just yelled!" says Katie. "I was afraid they'd put us out, you made us laugh so hard."

"Well," says Ralston, "I guess if they begin putting people out for that, I'd have to leave the troupe."

"It wouldn't be much of a show without you," says Ella.

"Well, all that keeps me in it is friendship for Ziggy," says Ralston. "I said to him last night, I says, 'Ziggy, I'm going to quit the troupe. I'm tired and I want to rest a wile.' So he says, 'Jim, don't quit or I'll have to close the troupe. I'll give you fifteen hundred a week to stay.' I'm getting a thousand now. But I says to him, I said, 'Ziggy, it ain't a question of money. What I want is a troupe of my own, where I get a chance to do serious work. I'm sick of making a monkey of myself in front of a bunch of saps from Nyack that don't appreciate no art but what's wrapped up in a stocking.' So he's promised that if I'll stick it out this year, he'll star me next season in a serious piece."

"Is he giving you the five hundred raise?" I ast him.

"I wouldn't take it," said Ralston. "I don't need money."

"At that, a person can live pretty cheap at this hotel," I says.

"I didn't move here because it was cheap," he said. "I moved here to get away from the pests—women that wants my autograph or my picture. And all they could say how much they enjoyed my work and how did I think up all them gags, and so forth. No real artist likes to talk about himself, especially to people that don't understand So that's the reason why I left the Ritz, so's I'd be left alone, not to save money. And I don't save no money, neither. I've got the best suite in the house—bedroom, bath and study."

"What do you study?" ast Kate.

"The parts I want to play," he says; "Hamlet and Macbeth and Richard."

"But you're a comedian," says Kate.

"It's just a stepping stone," said Ralston.

He'd finished his breakfast and got up.

"I must go to my study and work," he says. "We'll meet again."

"Yes, indeed," says Ella. "Do you always come right back here nights after the show?"

"When I can get away from the pests," he says.

"Well," says Ella, "suppose you come up to our rooms to-night and we'll have a bite to eat. And I think the husband can give you a little liquid refreshments if you ever indulge."

"Very little," he says. "What is your room number?"

So the Mrs. told him and he said he'd see us after the show that night, and walked out.

"Well," said Ella, "how do you like him?"

"I think he's wonderful!" says Katie. "I didn't have no idear he was so deep, wanting to play Hamlet."

"Pretty near all comedians has got that bug," I says.

"Maybe he's different when you know him better," said Ella.

"I don't want him to be different," says Kate.

"But he was so serious," said the Mrs. "He didn't say nothing funny."

"Sure he did," I says. "Didn't he say artists hate to talk about themselfs?"

Pretty soon the waiter come in with our lunch. He ast us if the other gentleman was coming back.

"No," said Ella. "He's through."

"He forgot his check," says the dish smasher.

"Oh, never mind!" says Ella. "We'll take care of that."

"Well," I says, "I guess the bird was telling the truth when he said he didn't need no money."

I and the gals spent the evening at a picture show and stopped at a delicatessen on the way home to stock up for the banquet. I had a quart and a pint of yearling rye, and a couple of bottles of McAllister that they'd fined me fifteen smackers apiece for and I wanted to save them, so I told Kate that I hoped her friend would get comical enough on the rye.

"He said he drunk very little," she reminded me.

"Remember, don't make him talk about himself," said the Mrs. "What we want is to have him feel at home, like he was with old friends, and then maybe he'll warm up. I hope we don't wake the whole hotel, laughing."

Well, Ralston showed about midnight. He'd remembered his date and apologized for not getting there before.

"I like to walk home from the theater," he says. "I get some of my funniest idears wile I walk."

I come to the conclusion later that he spent practically his whole life riding.

Ella's and my room wasn't no gymnasium for size and after the third drink, Ralston tried to get to the dresser to look at himself in the glass, and knocked a $30 vase for a corpse. This didn't go very big with the Mrs., but she forced a smile and would of accepted his apology if he'd made any. All he done was mumble something about cramped quarters. They was even more cramped when we set the table for the big feed, and it was my tough luck to have our guest park himself in the chair nearest the clothes closet, where my two bottles of Scotch had been put to bed. The fourth snifter finished the pint of rye and I said I'd get the other quart, but before I could stop her, Ella says:

"Let Mr. Ralston get it. It's right there by him."

So the next thing you know, James has found the good stuff and he comes out with both bottles of it.

"McAllister!" he says. "That's my favorite. If I'd knew you had that, I wouldn't of drank up all your rye."

"You haven't drank it all up," I says. "They's another bottle of it in there."

"It can stay there as long as we got this," he says, and helped himself to the corkscrew.

Well, amongst the knickknacks the gals had picked up at the delicatessen was a roast chicken and a bottle of olives, and at the time I thought Ralston was swallowing bones, stones and all.

It wasn't till the next day that we found all these keepsakes on the floor, along with a couple dozen assorted cigarette butts.

Katie's chorus gal friend had told her how funny the guy was when he'd had just the right number of shots, but I'd counted eight and begin to get discouraged before he started talking.

"My mother could certainly cook a chicken," he says.

"Is your mother living?" Kate ast him.

"No," he says. "She was killed in a railroad wreck. I'll never forget when I had to go and identify her. You wouldn't believe a person could get that mangled! No," he says, "my family's all gone. I never seen my father. He was in the pesthouse with smallpox when I was born and he died there. And my only sister died of jaundice. I can still——"

But Kate was scared we'd wake up the hotel, laughing, so she says: "Do you ever give imitations?"

"You mustn't make Mr. Ralston talk about himself," says Ella.

"Imitations of who?" said Ralston.

"Oh, other actors," said Katie.

"No," he says. "I leave it to the other actors to give imitations of me."

"I never seen none of them do it," says Kate.

"They all do it, but they don't advertise it," he says. "Every comic in New York is using my stuff."

"Oh!" said Ella. "You mean they steal your idears."

"Can't you go after them for it?" ast Katie.

"You could charge them with petit larceny," I said.

"I wouldn't be mean," said Ralston. "But they ain't a comic on the stage today that I didn't give him every laugh he's got."

"You ain't only been on the stage three or four years," I says. "How did Hitchcock and Ed Wynn and them fellas get by before they seen you?"

"They wasn't getting by," he says. "I'm the baby that put them on their feet. Take Hitchy. Hitchy come to me last spring and says, 'Jim, I've ran out of stuff. Have you got any notions I could use?' So I says, 'Hitchy, you're welcome to anything I got.' 'So I give him a couple of idears and they're the only laughs in his troupe. And you take Wynn. He opened up with a troupe that looked like a flop and one day I seen him on Broadway, wearing a long pan, and I says, 'What's the matter, Eddie?' And he brightened up and says, 'Hello, there, Jim! You're just the boy I want to see.' So I says, 'Well, Eddie, I'm only too glad to do anything I can.' So he says, 'I got a flop on my hands unlest I can get a couple of idears, and you're the baby that can give them to me.' So I said, 'All right, Eddie.' And I give him a couple of notions to work on and they made his show. And look at Stone! And Errol! And Jolson and Tinney! Every one of them come to me at one time another, hollering for help. 'Jim, give me a couple of notions!' 'Jim, give me a couple of gags!' And not a one of them went away empty-handed."

"Did they pay you?" ast Ella.

Ralston smiled.

"I wouldn't take no actor's money," he says. "They're all brothers to me. They can have anything I got, and I can have anything they got, only they haven't got nothing."

Well, I can't tell you all he said, as I was asleep part of the time. But I do remember that he was the one that had give Bert Williams the notion of playing coon parts, and learnt Sarah Bernhardt to talk French.

Along about four o'clock, when they was less than a pint left in the second McAllister bottle, he defied all the theater managers in New York.

"I ain't going to monkey with them much longer!" he says. "I'll let you folks in on something that'll cause a sensation on Broadway. I'm going to quit the Follies!"

We was all speechless.

"That's the big secret!" he says. "I'm coming out as a star under my own management and in a troupe wrote and produced by myself!"

"When?" ast Kate.

"Just as soon as I decide who I'm going to let in as part owner," said Ralston. "I've worked for other guys long enough! Why should I be satisfied with $800 a week when Ziegfeld's getting rich off me!"

"When did he cut you $200?" I says. "You was getting $1,000 last time I seen you,"

He didn't pay no attention.

"And why should I let some manager produce my play," he says, "and pay me maybe $1,200 a week when I ought to be making six or seven thousand!"

"Are you working on your play now?" Kate ast him.

"It's done," he says. "I'm just trying to make up my mind who's the right party to let in on it. Whoever it is, I'll make him rich."

"I've got some money to invest," says Katie. "Suppose you tell us about the play."

"I'll give you the notion, if you'll keep it to yourself," says Ralston. "It's a serious play with a novelty idear that'll be a sensation. Suppose I go down to my suite and get the script and read it to you."

"Oh, if you would!" says Kate.

"It'll knock you dead!" he says.

And just the thought of it was fatal to the author. He got up from his chair, done a nose dive acrost the table and laid there with his head in the chili sauce.

I called up the clerk and had him send up the night bellhop with our guest's key. I and the boy acted as pall bearers and got him to his "suite," where we performed the last sad rites. Before I come away I noticed that the "suite" was a ringer for Ella's and mine—a dinky little room with a bath. The "study" was prettily furnished with coat hangers.

When I got back to my room Katie'd ducked and the Mrs. was asleep, so I didn't get a chance to talk to them till we was in the restaurant at noon. Then I ast Kate if she'd figured out just what number drink it was that had started him being comical.

"Now listen," she says: "I don't think that Abbott girl ever met him in her life. Anyway, she had him all wrong. We expected he'd do stunts, like she said, but he ain't that kind that shows off or acts smart. He's too much of a man for that. He's a bigger man than I thought."

"I and the bellhop remarked that same thing," I says.

"And you needn't make fun of him for getting faint," says Katie. "I called him up a wile ago to find out how he was and he apologized and said they must of been something in that second bottle of Scotch."

So I says:

"You tell him they was, but they ain't."

Well, it couldn't of been the Scotch or no other brew that ruined me. Or if it was, it worked mighty slow. I didn't even look at a drink for three days after the party in our room. But the third day I felt rotten, and that night I come down with a fever. Ella got scared and called a doctor and he said it was flu, and if I didn't watch my step it'd be something worse. He advised taking me to a hospital and I didn't have pep enough to say no.

So they took me and I was pretty sick for a couple of weeks—too sick for the Mrs. to give me the news. And it's a wonder I didn't have a relapse when she finally did.

"You'll probably yelp when you hear this," she says. "I ain't crazy about it myself, but it didn't do me no good to argue at first and it's too late for argument now. Well, to begin with, Sis is in love with Ralston."

"What of it!" I said. "She's going through the city directory and she's just got to the R's."

"No, it's the real thing this time," said the Mrs. "Wait till you hear the rest of it. She's going on the stage!"

"I've got nothing against that," I says. "She's pretty enough to get by in the Follies chorus, and if she can earn money that way, I'm for it."

"She ain't going into no chorus," said Ella. "Ralston's quit the Follies and she's going in his show."

"The one he wrote?" I ast.

"Yes," said the Mrs.

"And who's going to put it on?" I ast her.

"That's it," she says. "They're going to put it on themself, Ralston and Sis. With Sis's money. She sold her bonds, fifty thousand dollars' worth."

"But listen," I says. "Fifty thousand dollars! What's the name of the play, Ringling's Circus?"

"It won't cost all that," said Ella. "They figure it'll take less than ten thousand to get started. But she insisted on having the whole thing in a checking account, where she can get at it. If the show's a big success in New York they're going to have a company in Chicago and another on the road. And Ralston says her half of the profits in New York ought to run round $5,000 a week. But anyway, she's sure of $200 a week salary for acting in it."

"Where did she get the idear she can act?" I says.

"She's always had it," said the Mrs., "and I think she made him promise to put her in the show before she agreed to back it. Though she says it's a wonderful investment! She won't be the leading woman, of course. But they's only two woman's parts and she's got one of them."

"Well," I said, "if she's going to play a sap and just acts normal, she'll be a sensation."

"I don't know what she'll be," says Ella. "All I know is that she's mad over Ralston and believes everything he says. And even if you hadn't of been sick we couldn't of stopped her."

So I ast what the play was like, but Ella couldn't tell me.

Ralston had read it out loud to she and Kate, but she couldn't judge from just hearing it that way. But Kate was tickled to death with it. And they'd already been rehearsing a week, but Sis hadn't let Ella see the rehearsals. She said it made her nervous.

"Ralston thinks the main trouble will be finding a theater," said the Mrs. "He says they's a shortage of them and the men that owns them won't want to let him have one on account of jealousy."

"Has the Follies flopped?" I ast her.

"No," she says, "but they've left town."

"They always do, this time of year," I said.

"That's what I thought," says the Mrs., "but Ralston says they'd intended to stay here all the year round, but when the news come out that he'd left, they didn't dast. He's certainly got faith in himself. He must have, to give up a $600 a week salary. That's what he says he was really getting."

"You say Katie's in love," I says. "How about him?"

"I don't know and she don't know," says Ella. "He calls her dearie and everything and holds her hands, but when they're alone together, he won't talk nothing but business. Still, as I say, he calls her dearie."

"Actors calls every gal that," I says. "It's because they can't remember names."

Well, to make a short story out of it, they had another couple weeks' rehearsals that we wasn't allowed to see, and they finally got a theater—the Olney. They had to guarantee a $10,000 business to get it. They didn't go to Atlantic City or nowheres for a tryout. They opened cold. And Ralston didn't tell nobody what kind of a show it was.

Of course he done what they generally always do on a first night. He sent out free passes to everybody that's got a dress suit, and they's enough of them in New York to pretty near fill up a theater. These invited guests is supposed to be for the performance wile it's going on. After it's through, they can go out and ride it all over the island.

Well, the rules wasn't exactly lived up to at "Bridget Sees a Ghost." On account of Ralston writing the play and starring in it, the gang thought it would be comical and they come prepared to laugh. It was comical all right, and they laughed. They didn't only laugh; they yelled. But they yelled in the wrong place.

The programme said it was "a Daring Drama in Three Acts." The three acts was what made it daring. It took nerve to even have one. In the first place, this was two years after the armistice and the play was about the war, and I don't know which the public was most interested in by this time—the war or Judge Parker.

Act 1 was in July, 1917. Ralston played the part of Francis Shaw, a captain in the American army. He's been married a year, and when the curtain goes up, his wife's in their New York home, waiting for him to come in from camp on his weekly leave. She sets reading the war news in the evening paper, and she reads it out loud, like people always do when they're alone, waiting for somebody. Pretty soon in comes Bridget, the Irish maid—our own dear Katie. And I wished you could of heard her brogue. And seen her gestures. What she reminded me most like was a gal in a home talent minstrels giving an imitation of Lew Fields playing the part of the block system on the New York Central. Her first line was, "Ain't der captain home yed?" But I won't try and give you her dialect.

"No," says Mrs. Shaw. "He's late." So Katie says better late than never, and the wife says, yes, but she's got a feeling that some day it'll be never; something tells her that if he ever goes to France, he won't come back. So Bridget says, "You been reading the war news again and it always makes you sad." "I hate wars!" says Mrs. Shaw, and that line got one of the biggest laughs.

After this they was a couple of minutes when neither of them could think of nothing to add, and then the phone rung and Bridget answered it. It was Capt. Shaw, saying he'd be there pretty soon; so Bridget goes right back to the kitchen to finish getting dinner, but she ain't no sooner than left the stage when Capt. Shaw struts in. He must of called up from the public booth on his front porch.

The audience had a tough time recognizing him without his comic make-up, but when they did they give him a good hand. Mrs. Shaw got up to greet him, but he brushed by her and come down to the footlights to bow. Then he turned and went back to his Mrs., saying "Maizie!" like this was the last place he expected to run acrost her. They kissed and then he ast her "Where is Bobbie, our dear little one?"—for fear she wouldn't know whose little one he meant. So she rung a bell and back come Bridget, and he says "Well, Bridget!" and Bridget says, "Well, it's the master!" This line was another riot. "Bring the little one, Bridget," says Mrs. Shaw, and the audience hollered again.

Wile Bridget was after the little one, the captain celebrated the reunion by walking round the room, looking at the pictures. Bridget brings the baby in and the captain uncovers its face and says, "Well, Bobbie!" Then he turns to his wife and says, "Let's see, Maizie. How old is he?" "Two weeks," says Maizie. "Two weeks!" says Captain Shaw, surprised. "Well," he says, "I hope by the time he's old enough to fight for the Stars and Stripes, they won't be no such a thing as war." So Mrs. Shaw says, "And I hope his father won't be called on to make the supreme sacrifice for him and we others that must stay home and wait. I sometimes think that in wartime, it's the women and children that suffers most. Take him back to his cozy cradle, Bridget. We mothers must be careful of our little ones. Who knows when the kiddies will be our only comfort!" So Bridget beat it out with the little one and I bet he hated to leave all the gayety.

"Well," says Shaw to his wife, "and what's the little woman been doing?"

"Just reading," she says, "reading the news of this horrible war. I don't never pick up the paper but what I think that some day I'll see your name amongst the dead."

"Well," says the captain bravely, "they's no danger wile I stay on U.S. soil. But only for you and the little one, I would welcome the call to go Over There and take my place in the battle line. The call will come soon, I believe, for they say France needs men." This rumor pretty near caused a riot in the audience and Ralston turned and give us all a dirty look.

Then Bridget come in again and said dinner was ready, and Shaw says, "It'll seem funny to set down wile I eat." Which was the first time I ever knew that army captains took their meals off the mantelpiece.

Wile the Shaws was out eating, their maid stayed in the living room, where she'd be out of their way. It seems that Ralston had wrote a swell speech for her to make in this spot, about what a tough thing war is, to come along and separate a happy young couple like the Shaws that hadn't only been married a year. But the speech started "This is terrible!" and when Bridget got that much of it out, some egg in the gallery hollered "You said a mouthful, kid!" and stopped the show.

The house finally quieted down, but Katie was dumb for the first time in her life. She couldn't say the line that was the cue for the phone to ring, and she had to go over and answer a silent call. It was for the captain, and him and his wife both come back on the stage.

"Maizie," he says, after he'd hung up, "it's came! That was my general! We sail for France in half an hour!"

"O husband!" says Maizie. "This is the end!"

"Nonsense!" says Shaw with a brave smile. "This war means death for only a small per cent, of our men."

"And almost no captains," yells the guy in the gallery.

Shaw gets ready to go, but she tells him to wait till she puts on her wraps; she'll go down to the dock and see him off.

"No, darling," he says. "Our orders is secret. I can't give you the name of our ship or where we're sailing from."

So he goes and she flops on the couch w'ining because he wouldn't tell her whether his ship left from Times Square or Grand Central.

They rung the curtain down here to make you think six days has passed. When it goes up again, Maizie's setting on the couch, holding the little one. Pretty soon Bridget comes in with the evening paper.

"They's a big headline, mum," she says. "A troopship has been torpedoed."

Well, when she handed her the paper, I could see the big headline. It said, "Phillies Hit Grimes Hard." But Maizie may of had a bet on Brooklyn. Anyway, she begin trembling and finally fell over stiff. So Bridget picked up the paper and read it out loud:

"Amongst the men lost was Capt. P. Shaw of New York."

Down went the curtain again and the first act was over, and some jokesmith in the audience yelled "Author! Author!"

"He's sunk!" said the egg in the gallery.

Well, Maizie was the only one in the whole theater that thought Shaw was dead. The rest of us just wished it. Still you couldn't blame her much for getting a wrong idear, as it was Nov. 11, 1918—over a year later—when the second act begins, and she hadn't heard from him in all that time. It wasn't never brought out why. Maybe he'd forgot her name or maybe it was Burleson's fault, like everything else.

The scene was the same old living room and Maizie was setting on the same old couch, but she was all dressed up like Elsie Ferguson. It comes out that she's expecting a gentleman friend, a Mr. Thornton, to dinner. She asks Bridget if she thinks it would be wrong of her to accept the guy the next time he proposed. He's ast her every evening for the last six months and she can't stall him much longer. So Bridget says it's all right if she loves him, but Maizie don't know if she loves him or not, but he looks so much like her late relic that she can't hardly tell the difference and besides, she has got to either marry or go to work, or her and the little one will starve. They's a knock at the door and Thornton comes in. Him and the absent captain looks as much alike as two brothers, yours and mine. Bridget ducks and Thornton proposes. Maizie says, "Before I answer, I must tell you a secret. Captain Shaw didn't leave me all alone. I have a little one, a boy." "Oh, I love kiddies," says Thornton, "Can I see him?" So she says it's seven o'clock and the little one's supposed to of been put to bed, but she has Bridget go get him.

The little one's entrance was the sensation of this act. In Act 1 he was just three or four towels, but now Bridget can't even carry him acrost the stage, and when she put him on his feet, he comes up pretty near to her shoulder. And when Thornton ast him would he like to have a new papa, he says, "Yes, because my other papa's never coming back."

Well, they say a woman can't keep a secret, but if Thornton had been nosing round for six months and didn't know till now that they was a spanker like Bobbie in the family circle, I wouldn't hardly call Maizie the town gossip.

After the baby'd went back to read himself to sleep and Mrs. Shaw had yessed her new admirer, Bridget dashed in yelling that the armistice was signed and held up the evening paper for Maizie and Thornton to see. The great news was announced in code. It said: "Phillies Hit Grimes Hard." And it seemed kind of silly to not come right out and say "Armistice Signed!" Because as I recall, even we saps out here in South Bend had knew it since three o'clock that morning.

The last act was in the same place, on Christmas Eve, 1918.

Maizie and her second husband had just finished doing up presents for the little one. We couldn't see the presents, but I suppose they was giving him a cocktail shaker and a shaving set. Though when he come on the stage you could see he hadn't aged much since Act 2. He hadn't even begin to get bald.

Thornton and the Mrs. went off somewheres and left the kid alone, but all of a sudden the front door opened and in come old Cap Shaw, on crutches. He seen the kid and called to him. "Who are you?" says the little one. "I'm Santa Claus," says the Cap, "and I've broughten you a papa for Christmas." "I don't want no papa," says Bobbie. "I've just got a new one." Then Bridget popped in and seen "the master" and hollered, "A ghost!"

So he got her calmed down and she tells him what's came off. "It was in the paper that Capt. F. Shaw of New York was lost," she says. "It must of been another Capt. F. Shaw!" he says.

"It's an odd name," hollered the guy in the gallery.

The Captain thinks it all over and decides it's his move. He makes Bridget promise to never tell that she seen him and he says good-by to she and the kid and goes out into the night.

Maizie comes in, saying she heard a noise and what was it? Was somebody here? "Just the boy with the evening paper," says Bridget. And the cat's got Bobbie's tongue. And Maizie don't even ask for the paper. She probably figured to herself it was the old story; that Grimes was still getting his bumps.

Well, I wished you could of read what the papers wrote up about the show. One of them said that Bridget seen a ghost at the Olney theater last night and if anybody else wanted to see it, they better go quick because it wouldn't be walking after this week. Not even on crutches. The mildest thing they said about Ralston was that he was even funnier than when he was in the Follies and tried to be. And they said the part of Bridget was played by a young actress that they hoped would make a name for herself, because Ralston had probably called her all he could think of.

We waited at the stage door that night and when Kate come out, she was crying. Ralston had canned her from the show.

"That's nothing to cry about," I says. "You're lucky! It's just like as if a conductor had put you off a train a couple of minutes before a big smash-up."

The programme had been to all go somewheres for supper and celebrate the play's success. But all Katie wanted now was to get in a taxi and go home and hide.

On the way, I ast her how much she was in so far.

"Just ten thousand," she says.

"Ten thousand!" I said. "Why, they was only one piece of scenery and that looked like they'd bought it secondhand from the choir boys' minstrels. They couldn't of spent one thousand, let alone ten."

"We had to pay the theater a week's rent in advance," she says. "And Jimmy give five thousand to a man for the idear."

"The idear for what?" I ast.

"The idear for the play," she said.

"That stops me!" I says. "This baby furnishes idears for all the good actors in the world, but when he wants one for himself, he goes out and pays $5,000 for it. And if he got a bargain, you're Mrs. Fiske."

"Who sold him the idear?" ast Ella.

"He wouldn't tell me," says Kate.

"Ponzi," I said.

Ralston called Kate up the next noon and made a date with her at the theater. He said that he was sorry he'd been rough. Before she went I ast her to give me a check for the forty thousand she had left so's I could buy back some of her bonds.

"I haven't got only $25,000," she says. "I advanced Jimmy fifteen thousand for his own account, so's he wouldn't have to bother me every time they was bills to meet."

So I said: "Listen: I'll go see him with you and if he don't come clean with that money, I'll knock him deader'n his play."

"Thank you!" she says. "I'll tend to my own affairs alone."

She come back late in the afternoon, all smiles.

"Everything's all right," she said. "I give him his choice of letting me be in the play or giving me my money."

"And which did he choose?" I ast her.

"Neither one," she says. "We're going to get married."

"Bridget" went into the ashcan Saturday night and the wedding come off Monday. Monday night they left for Boston, where the Follies was playing. Kate told us they'd took Ralston back at the same salary he was getting before.

"How much is that?" I ast her.

"Four hundred a week," she says.

Well, two or three days after they'd left, I got up my nerve and says to the Mrs.:

"Do you remember what we moved to the Big Town for? We done it to see Life and get Katie a husband. Well, we got her a kind of a husband and I'll tell the world we seen Life. How about moseying back to South Bend?"

"But we haven't no home there now."

"Nor we ain't had none since we left there," I says. "I'm going down and see what's the first day we can get a couple of lowers."

"Get uppers if it's quicker," says the Mrs.

So here we are, really enjoying ourselfs for the first time in pretty near two years. And Katie's in New York, enjoying herself, too, I suppose. She ought to be, married to a comedian. It must be such fun to just set and listen to him talk.

The End

About the Author

Ring W. Lardner (1885–1933) was one of the most famous and widely read American writers of the early twentieth century. His weekly column for the Bell Syndicate was read from coast to coast, and he published short fiction, essays, and sports writing in leading magazines and newspapers. A native of Niles, Michigan, Lardner is most closely associated with Chicago, having covered the 1920 Democratic National Convention and the infamous 1919 Chicago Black Sox scandal for the *Chicago Tribune*. Known primarily as a baseball writer and humorist, he possessed a sharp ear for dialogue and a razor-sharp wit, which he used to critique the ambitions and eccentricities of everyday Americans. His work includes the satirical collections *You Know Me Al* (1916), *Gullible's Travels, Etc.* (1918), and *The Real Dope* (1919), the short story cycle *The Big Town* (1921), the short story collections *How to Write Short Stories with Samples* (1924), *The Love Nest and Other Stories* (1926), and *Round Up* (1929), and the hit Broadway play *June Moon* (1929, with George S. Kaufman). He was posthumously awarded the J.G. Taylor Spink Award from the Baseball Writers' Association of America in 1964.